人性深邃
之拜訪
美國近代經典短篇小說選

涂成吉———編著

自 序

　　小說藉由情節之戲劇化及角色上性格的生動，一直是應用英語系或英文系善用之英語教學媒介。蓋有人性始有文學，有人性始有小說，正因人性之深不可測，各人性格之千變萬化，如同指間的紋路，小說正是發掘此一人心無底之多樣生命故事，讓讀者能於欣賞，但有脈絡，最終留有動人的餘韻下，直接探訪人性的深邃。

　　大底言，西方現代小說的成形，源始十八世紀末所開啟之「浪漫主義」思潮，當知識份子開始質疑啟蒙時代所推崇理性與進步、秩序與和諧的這些想法，轉而強調個人心靈、獨特性與想像力的重要時；浪漫主義等於正式宣告人類始祖亞當、夏娃因對上帝「說謊」，開啟西方對「人性本惡」共識的結束。而當人類由「神本」的迷信，邁進「人本」的自信，人性取得全面的解放時，不但人情的正面：善、智慧與感性，取得認同；同時對人性的負面：自私、妒嫉與憎恨，也能包容探索，這是西方大不同中國儒家人性本善，一昧去惡存善的固執，而讓西方小說的內容更客觀接近人性寬廣與複雜的真實。

　　此外，「文史不分」，小說也能跨領域與社會科學連結，兼具歷史文化的深入，從小說中見證歷史，看到小說背後的社會意義，打破過去文學課程純文學性的討論，不單有助學子分析、批判思考的能力，同時培養人文關懷的精神，才是小說終究影響之所在。

　　大體而言，現代小說之體系發展也是與時代環境平行互動與變遷下的人心反映。十九世紀中葉以後，工商革命創造了現代資本文明，當人們以為找到了人類最公平與理想之生活方式時，小說文人卻視功利放任的競逐，是以自然為豁，侵蝕人心本性最駭者，又興起「寫實主義」與「自然主義」，轉而筆觸人事真實題材，關注社會周遭變化。待二十世紀，隨著社會進步的更快與人際多元複雜，人又對個人存在價值產生懷疑，這以「自我」為創作基礎，發掘人的內心活動，出現了頹廢派、荒誕派、象徵主義、虛無主義、意識流等小說，使小說的本質發生了變異，此乃「現代主義」崛起。

　　本書之編構由此，過濾與精選了主要以美國小說家為代表，分具浪漫、寫實、自然主義與現代主義，風格明確、主題突出的二十篇經典短篇小說，再加以要言不繁的作者短評與作品分析，除文學的概念外，也旁及美國文學、歷史、文化的解說與認識。如詹姆士・古柏《日蝕》，可謂美國本土文學拓荒之作，使美國文學從模仿英國及歐陸的風格中，脫穎開創了美國文藝復興。霍桑《年輕的布朗大爺》與愛倫・坡《弗德馬先生案的真相》都是美國浪漫主義初期，探索人性「善、惡」對立的標準之作，惟愛倫・坡是以黑色劇的娛樂效果呈現，而梅爾維爾《提琴手》一文則探討人性中不變的宿命式悲劇，簡單道出宿命的形成，不過是個人過度的堅持，背後，霍桑與梅爾維爾其實都直接挑戰了美國賴以立國的清教價值衝突。

當十九世紀，人類進入工業社會，狄更斯正是這資本文明勢利歪風下，人道寫實的先驅。為美國後世小說所效仿。他《兒童的故事》宛如一幅人生畫卷，兼具幽默、批判與溫暖。

而史蒂芬・克蘭小說《海上扁舟》、畢爾斯《梟河橋記事》與傑克・倫敦《生火》分別置個人在大海、戰爭及北國冰天雪地中，顯現原始人性，探討人心惟危的本質力量，是美國最突出的三篇自然主義代表之作。

有關現代主義短篇小說純文學技巧、觀念之展示：則有海明威《白象似的群山》之「冰山理論」，感受小說文字無聲勝有聲的弦外之音；莫泊桑悲觀厭世，卻用文筆戲謔、結局意外方式呈現，他《項鍊》是美國人最愛短篇小說，也深深影響日後美國小說家歐・亨利寫作策略──「歐・亨利式結局」──如果你喜歡享受surprise或跌碎眼鏡的快感，歐・亨利《最後一片葉子》應該是不會使你失望的選擇；而王爾德《自私的巨人》告訴你文章之唯美有時不如淒美來得動人；法蘭克・史塔頓《美女還是老虎？》則說明「兩難」的選擇是小說最有張力的創作法寶。至於現代主義中，向人性內心更潛深處探索的「意識流」派運用，自不可缺席，特別以喬伊斯《伊芙琳》和伍爾芙《一間鬼屋》兩篇簡明「意識流」佳作，向此一文學大殿扣門。

再就小說精準抓住一個社會當時經濟、政治及道德的歷史與意義的語言密碼而言，馬克・吐溫《好小孩的故事》、威廉‧福克納《給愛蜜麗的玫瑰》充分表現美國地域文化中——大西部的純樸、粗獷及南方的封閉、懷舊調性。凱特‧蕭邦《一小時的故事》深刻暗諷十九世紀，美國女性社會地位之卑微；史考特‧費茲傑羅《一個酗酒案例》無疑是美國二十世紀，二〇年代下「失落的一代」的奢華，以至三〇年代，美國跌進經濟谷底的歷史縮影；最終，薛吾德‧安德森《林中之死》則是就二十世紀資本文明生活下的省思，企圖了解生命與死亡的奧秘，找尋人在每天平凡生活中的美麗與意義。

　　最後，本書的編選除是為應英系學子在小說的課程學習上，有一更快及基礎性的認識外，也是給我的女兒——敏，她是讓我看得到時間的人，昨天的小女孩，轉眼，今夏已為臺大新鮮人，每天看她興奮於學問與未來的憧憬中，希望這二十篇的小說故事，能帶給她一些客觀看待人性萬般的啟示！

民國一〇一年八月於內湖

CONTENTS

詹姆士・古柏《日蝕》
——美國本土文學拓荒者

詹姆士・古柏
(James F. Cooper, 1789-1851)

小說特徵

美國本土自然風光、拓荒者
與印地安人戰爭的邊疆故事

The affairs of life embrace a multitude of interests, and he who reasons in any one of them, is a visionary.

-James F. Cooper

生活的事務包含著多重趣味，凡事以理性看待，則成虛幻。
——詹姆士・古柏

作者短評

詹姆士・古柏（James F. Cooper），1789年，生於紐澤西，家世富裕，父親是大地主、國會議員，一歲，移居紐約古柏鎮，這由他父親以家族為名所建立城鎮。古柏十三歲就讀於耶魯大學，卻因為頻頻惡作劇，像是炸掉同學的房門，教驢子跳到老師背上，而被踢出校門，由此可見古柏放蕩不拘的個性。之後，古柏上了商船，作了水手；十八歲，正式加入美國海軍。古柏成名之作《皮襪的故事》（*The Leatherstocking Tales*），是由《拓荒著》（*The Pioneers,* 1823）、《最後的摩希根人》（*The Last of the Mohicans,* 1826）、《大草原》（*The Prairie,* 1827）、《開路人》（*The Pathfinder,* 1840）、《殺鹿人》（*The Deerslayer,* 1841）五部作品的合成，系列描寫美國殖民地時期，英、法軍隊在北美洲引發的殖民戰爭，與獨立拓荒時代，西部移民艱苦生存的故事，以及印地安族群被滅絕的悲慘遭遇。其中，最耳熟能詳代表美國本土文學開山之作——《最後的摩希根人》（*The Last of the Mohicans*），好萊塢也改拍成電影《大地英豪》，由丹尼爾戴路易斯（Daniel Day Lewis）主演。敘述主角是一位白人，卻是由印地安人撫養長大，之後，轉而對抗來自英、法殖民的統治殺戮，隱喻新大陸的善與舊世界的惡，文中除表達美國本土印地安人對自然的尊重與共生的和諧，譬如文中印地安人對所獵殺動物，會表達惺惺相惜之意，同時也暗表對印地安人不停遭受白人移民的滅族殺害，導致族群消失的遺憾。

古柏，1826年，因發展寫作事業，而移居歐洲，直到1833年，才返鄉定居古柏鎮的Otsego Hall，期間一度改採政治內容的寫作，卻不受歡迎，才繼續原來拓荒者與印地安人戰爭的邊疆故事，而完成後續之《開路人》與《殺鹿人》。1851年古柏在家鄉過世。

作品分析

美國自1776年獨立建國起，至十九世紀中，不過百年，財富與國力就有獨步全球的氣勢；惟文學上，美國人民仍醉心英國進口的文學書刊與小說，惟英國作家所見是瞻，這般文學依賴現象，無怪1802年，英國文學批評家希尼史密斯（Sydney Smith）寫道：「在本世紀，誰讀過一本美國人寫的書？誰看過美國人寫的歌劇？誰曾觀賞過美國人所作一幅畫或一件雕刻？」，這一俐落話語雖失之尖酸，卻也深刻道白當時美國文學成就上的貧乏自卑。

在感慨美國雖然政治獨立，卻仍然是英國文學附庸的事實，詹姆士・古柏可謂是第一位能吸引國內讀者轉注美國本土文學的拓荒之士。而使古柏創作，有別歐洲舊大陸者，正是他引用新大陸之壯闊山川、原始林木及原住民印地安人的本土素材，作為他創作內容和靈感。

古柏成長於紐約州中部，幼年即見識西部拓展甘苦，親睹向西部拓荒中，移民與印地安人及大自然搏鬥感人過程，而生迷戀之情，轉而以西部拓荒者與印地安人生活為小說題材，探討個人與自然關係，雕塑美國人獨立、自由、理想及道德形象，也因為古柏的成功，才激勵1830年代之後，一群來自美國東北部新英格蘭地區（New England）的文學人士如愛默生（R. W. Emerson）、霍桑（Nathaniel Hawthorne）、惠特曼（Walt Whiteman）等許多卓越的文學家和思想家，發起國家文學解放運動，造就美國本土民族文學理論——「超越主義」[1]（Transcendentalism）的誕生，使美國文學從模仿英國及歐洲大陸的風格中，脫穎開創了美國文藝復興，幫助美國人完成了文學立國之夢。

本文所選古柏短篇小說《日蝕》，其實正是古柏回憶1806年6月16日，發生在他北美故鄉Otsego的日蝕奇景，文中描述了家鄉的青山、湖泊、樹林、田野、峭壁與洞穴，一切有如「老友臉龐般親切」，而村鎮的精神象徵是一棵枯萎無枝的老松有如「自由的旗桿」，作者總是以此認出如今荒蕪的昔日森林所在。而村民在期待日蝕的日子中，似乎為平淡的生活增添一絲興奮，古柏敘述了許多日蝕前的珍奇自然現象如露水不斷的降下，萬鳥不啼，蝙蝠盤旋，天象上，星星更見閃爍，閃電、濃雲的出現，當月亮將日光搶奪，每天村鎮午時的熱浪瞬間消去，氣溫驟降，當光明重返山谷，內心的感動與振奮，又讓親

---

[1] 超越主義（Transcendentalism）是十九世紀，美國本土文人響應浪漫文學運動下而生之國家民族文學運動，發起人愛默生為超越文學定義：「超越主義者主張心靈主義聯想，相信奇蹟、啓發與極度喜悅。我們對先人所言，常不假思索的採信，怯於自我實現。超越主義者是決不流於世俗，只作自己。」

身體會者有股莫名的激動，古柏將之比擬「基督的回聲，輕呼我們心靈，賦予這自然現象神秘的心理啟示」，讓古柏深刻體會照造物者之神奇與最深的敬畏。

文選閱讀

The Eclipse

by James F. Cooper

THE eclipse of the sun occurred in the summer of 1806, on Monday, the 16th of June. Its greatest depth of shadow fell upon the American continent, some- where about the latitude of 42 deg. I was then on a visit to my parents, at the home of my family, among the Highlands of Otsego, in that part of the country where the eclipse was most impressive. My recollections of the great event, and the incidents of the day, are as vivid as if they had occurred but yesterday.

Lake Otsego, the headwaters of the Susquehanna, lies as nearly as possible in latitude 42 deg. The village, which is the home of my family, is beautifully situated at the foot of the lake, in a valley lying between two nearly parallel ranges of heights, quite mountainous in character. The Susquehanna, a clear and rapid stream, flowing from the southeastern shore of the lake, is crossed by a high wooden bridge, which divides the main street of the little town from the lawns and meadows on the eastern bank of the river. Here were all the materials that could be desired, lake, river, mountain, wood, and the dwellings of man, to give full effect to the varied movement of light and shadow through that impressive day.

Throughout the belt of country to be darkened by the eclipse, the whole population were in a state of almost anxious expectation for weeks before the event. On the eve of the 16th of June, our family circle could think or talk of little else. I had then a father and four brothers living, and as we paced the broad hall of the house, or sat about the family board, our conversation turned almost entirely upon the movements of planets and comets, occultations and eclipses. We were all exulting in the feeling that a grand and extraordinary spectacle awaited us--a spectacle which millions then living could never behold. There may have been a tinge of selfishness in the feeling that we were thus favored beyond others.

And the first movement in the morning was to the open window-- again to examine the sky. When I rose from my bed, in the early morning, I found the heavens serene, and cloudless. Day had dawned, but the shadows of night were still lingering over the valley. For a moment, my eye rested on the familiar view--the limpid lake, with its setting of luxuriant woods and farms, its graceful bay and varied points, the hills where every cliff and cave and glen had been trodden a thousand times by my boyish feet--all this was dear to me as the face of a friend. And it appeared as if the landscape, then lovely in summer beauty, were about to assume something of dignity hitherto unknown--were not the shadows of a grand eclipse to fall upon every wave and branch within a few hours! There was one object in the landscape which a stranger would probably have overlooked, but it was familiar to every eye in the village, and endowed by our people with the honors of an ancient landmark--the tall gray trunk of a dead and branchless pine, which had been standing on the crest of the eastern hill, at the time of the foundation of the village, and which was still erect, though rocked since then by a thousand storms. To my childish fancy, it had seemed an imaginary flag-staff, or the "liberty pole" of some former generation; but now, as I traced the familiar line of the tall trunk, in its peculiar shade of silvery gray, it became to the eye of the young sailor the mast of some phantom ship. I remember greeting it with a smile, as this was the first glance of recognition given to the old ruin of the forest since my return.

But an object of far higher interest suddenly attracted my eye. I discovered a star--a solitary star--twinkling dimly in a sky. There was absolutely no other object visible in the heavens--cloud there was none, not even the lightest vapor. That lonely star excited a vivid interest in my mind. I continued at the window gazing, and losing myself in a sort of day-dream. That star was a heavenly body, it was known to be a planet, and my mind was filling itself with images of planets and suns...

Soon the sun himself rose into view. I caught a glimpse of fiery light glowing among the branches of the forest, on the eastern mountain. I watched, as I had done a hundred times before, the flushing of the skies, the gradual illuminations of the different hills, crowned with an undulating and ragged outline of pines, nearly two hundred feet in height, the golden light gliding silently down the breast of the western mountains, and opening clearer views of grove and field, until lake, valley, and village lay smiling in one cheerful glow of warm sunshine.

As yet there was no change perceptible in the sunlight falling upon lake and mountain; the familiar scene wore its usual smiling aspect, bright and glowing as on other days of June. The people, however, were now crowding into the streets--their usual labors were abandoned and all faces were turned upward. Gradually a fifth, and even a fourth, of the sun's disc became obscured, and still the unguarded eye could not endure the flood of light--it was only with the colored glass that we could note the progress of the phenomenon. The noon-day heat, however, began to lessen, and something of the coolness of early morning returned to the valley.

A great change had taken place. The trees on the distant heights had lost their verdure and their airy character. The lake wore a lurid aspect, very unusual. All living creatures seemed thrown into a state of agitation. The birds were fluttering to and fro, in great excitement; they seemed to mistrust that this was not the gradual approach of evening, and were undecided in their movements. Even the dogs--honest creatures--became uneasy, and drew closer to their masters. The eager, joyous look of interest and curiosity, which earlier in the morning had appeared in almost every countenance, was now changed to an expression of wonder or anxiety or thoughtfulness, according to the individual character.

Every house now gave up its tenants. As the light failed more and more with every passing second, the children came flocking about their mothers in terror. The women themselves were looking about uneasily for their husbands. The American wife is more apt than any other to turn with affectionate confidence to the stronger arm for support. The men were very generally silent and grave. Many a laborer left his employment to be near his wife and children, as the dimness and darkness increased.

I once more took my position beside my father and my brothers, before the gates of our own grounds. The sun lay a little obliquely to the south and east, in the most favorable position possible for observation. I remember to have examined, in vain, the whole dusky canopy in search of a single cloud. It was one of those entirely unclouded days, less rare in America than in Europe. The steadily waning light, the gradual approach of darkness, became the more impressive as we observed this absolutely transparent state of the heavens. The birds, which a quarter of an hour earlier had been fluttering about in great agitation, seemed now convinced that night was at hand. Swallows were dimly seen dropping into the chimneys, the martins returned to their little boxes, the pigeons flew home to their dove-cots, and through the open door of a small barn we saw the fowls going to roost.

The usual flood of sunlight had now become so much weakened, that we could look upward long, and steadily, without the least pain. The sun appeared like a young moon of three or four days old, though of course with a larger and more brilliant crescent. Looking westward a moment, a spark appeared to glitter before my eye. For a second I believed it to be an optical illusion, but in another instant I saw it plainly to be a star. One after another they came into view, more rapidly than in the evening twilight, until perhaps fifty stars appeared to us, in a broad, dark zone of the heavens, crowning the pines on the western mountain. This wonderful vision of the stars, during the noontide hours of day, filled the spirit with singular sensations.

Suddenly one of my brothers shouted aloud, "The moon!" Quicker than thought, my eye turned eastward again, and there floated the moon, distinctly apparent, to a degree that was almost fearful. The spherical form, the character, the dignity, the substance of the planet, were clearly revealed as I have never beheld them before, or since. It looked grand, dark, majestic, and mighty, as it thus proved its power to rob us entirely of the sun's rays. We are all but larger children. In daily life we judge of objects by their outward aspect. We are accustomed to think of the sun, and also of the moon, as sources of light, almost spiritual, in their essence. But the positive material nature of the moon was now revealed to our senses, with a force of conviction, a clearness of perception, that changed all our usual ideas in connection with the planet. This was but a vast mass of obvious matter had interposed between the sun above us and the earth on which we stood. The passage of two ships at sea, sailing on opposite courses, is scarcely more obvious than this movement of one world before another. Darkness like that of early night now fell upon the village.

I was recalled by a familiar and insignificant incident, the dull tramp of hoofs on the village bridge. A few cows, believing that night had overtaken them, were coming homeward from the wild open pastures about the village. And no wonder the kindly creatures were deceived, the darkness was now much deeper than the twilight which usually turns their faces homeward; the dew was falling perceptibly, as much so as at any hour of the previous night, and the coolness was so great that the thermometer must have fallen many degrees from the great heat of the morning. The lake, the hills, and the buildings of the little town were swallowed up in the darkness. The absence of the usual lights in the dwellings rendered the obscurity still more impressive. All labor had ceased, and the hushed voices of the people only broke the absolute stillness by subdued whispering tones.

"Hist! The whippoorwill!" whispered a friend near me; and at the same moment, as we listened in profound silence, we distinctly heard from the eastern bank of the river the wild, plaintive note of that solitary bird of night, slowly repeated at intervals. The song of the summer birds, so full in June, had entirely ceased for the last half hour. A bat came flitting about our heads. Many stars were now visible, though not in sufficient number to lessen the darkness. At one point only in the far distant northern horizon, something of the brightness of dawn appeared to linger.

At twelve minutes past eleven, the moon stood revealed in its greatest distinctness--a vast black orb, so nearly obscuring the sun that the face of the great luminary was entirely and absolutely darkened, though a corona of rays of light appeared beyond. The gloom of night was upon us. A breathless intensity of interest was felt by all. The peaceful rainbow, the heavy clouds of a great storm, the vivid flash of electricity, the falling meteor, the beautiful lights of the aurora borealis, fickle as the play of fancy,--these never fail to fix the attention with something of a peculiar feeling, different in character from that with which we observe any spectacle on the earth. Connected with all grand movements in the skies there seems an instinctive sense of inquiry, of anxious expectation; akin to awe, which may possibly be traced to the echoes of grand Christian prophecies, whispering to our spirits, and endowing the physical sight with some mysterious mental prescience. In looking back to that impressive hour, such now seem to me the feelings of the youth making one of that family group, all apparently impressed with a sensation of the deepest awe--I speak with certainty--a clearer view than I had ever yet had of the majesty of the Almighty.

Thus far the sensation created by this majestic spectacle had been one of humiliation and awe. It seemed as if the great Father of the Universe had visibly, and almost palpably, veiled his face in wrath. But, appalling as the withdrawal of light had been, most glorious, most sublime, was its restoration! It seemed to speak directly to our spirits, with full assurance of protection, of gracious mercy, and of that Divine love which has produced all the glorious combinations of matter for our enjoyment.

Men who witness any extraordinary spectacle together, are apt, in after-times, to find a pleasure in conversing on its impressions. But I do not remember to have ever heard a single being freely communicative on the subject of his individual feelings at the most solemn moment of the eclipse. It would seem as if sensations were aroused too closely connected with the constitution of the spirit to be irreverently and familiarly discussed. I shall only say that I have passed a varied and eventful life, that it has been my fortune to see earth, heavens, ocean, and man in most of their aspects; but never have I beheld any spectacle which so plainly manifested the majesty of the Creator, or so forcibly taught the lesson of humility to man as a total eclipse of the sun.

2 霍桑《年輕的布朗大爺》
——掙脫人性枷鎖之浪漫主義大師

小說特徵

人本、反清教、善與惡之對立

納撒尼爾・霍桑
(Nathaniel Hawthorne, 1804-1864)

There is evil in every human heart, which may retain latent, perhaps, through the whole life; but circumstances may rouse it to activity.

-Nathaniel Hawthorne

每一個人的內心都有邪惡，也許會潛伏一生，也可能有被喚醒行動的時候。

——納撒尼爾・霍桑

作者短評

　　納撒尼爾・霍桑（Nathaniel Hawthorne），1804年，出生於美國麻塞諸塞州賽倫（Salem），全鎮充滿濃厚之清教氣息，霍桑全家皆為清教徒[2]（Puritans），教條生活的一成不變，使霍桑作品充滿反抗清教意識。

　　清教徒重視道德與努力工作，一切以教義為尊，壓制人心，這也是何以清教思想總予美國人一股愛、憎交雜的情緒，愛的是它堅毅執著的宗教情懷，孕育出美國人民傳統的理想性格；憎的也是他一絲不苟，不容挑戰的價值權威，將人性束縛在他如鋼鐵般的宗教紀律之中。清教徒排斥感情，崇尚禁慾簡樸，以教義為生活指導，不但迫害異己，甚至連婦女在街上微笑都要處以監禁，兒童嬉戲也要加以鞭笞，採取的是政教合一的神道政權形式，霍桑家族先後在迫害桂格（Quaker）教派的「獵巫案」（witch hunting）中扮演過不光彩的角色，家族的這一段歷史使長大成人後的霍桑在心理上始終懷有愧罪感，清教主義的幽暗背景，於人性和心靈的壓制和摧殘，對霍桑的思想及創作皆產生了極大的影響，被譽為美國十九世紀最具影響的浪漫主義小說家。

2　英國國王亨利八世，1534年，加入宗教革命運動，自立英國國教（Church of England），但亨利八世動機只是因個人婚姻問題不得羅馬教皇祝福而反舊教，故目的達成後，對改革舊教一事自敷衍了事，而堅持去除舊教於國教者則被以清教徒稱之。

1842年，霍桑移居康考特（Concord），結識了美國本土版的浪漫主義——「超越主義」（Transcendentalism）作家如：愛默生、梅爾維爾、梭羅等人，「超越主義」作家由於對人性有更高信心，加以康考特也正處清教大本營新英格蘭的麻州，這使喀爾文清教思想（Calvinist Puritanism），勢所難免地成了超越文學作家首當其衝的挑戰。文學創作上，超越主義也的確針對清教思想於個人自由的壓抑，莫不口誅筆伐，相信人格一如神格，可止於至善；這使霍桑一度參加烏托邦式布魯克農場（Brook Farm）的生活實驗。

霍桑抨擊清教的食古不化和教會虛偽，慣用象徵手法，揭示人物內心衝突和心理描寫，作品往往帶有濃厚的宗教氣氛和神祕色彩，霍桑和愛倫・坡一樣喜好運用一些超自然的元素，並且同樣具有美學而不是宗教的基礎，但不同愛倫・坡小說上強調「恐怖娛樂」的效果，霍桑總是更關注倫理和哲學方面的思考和探索，這就使他的作品總是蘊含着令人回味不盡的深邃哲理，故文學史家常把他列為浪漫主義作家，長篇小說《紅字》公認是霍桑最成功之作，塑造個人內心與外在（清教）價值的反抗與轉變，其探索之深入，文筆之洗鍊，媲美二十世紀初期的意識流小說，霍桑在美國文學史上的地位也更為確定。

南北戰爭爆發後，霍桑的身體每況愈下，1864年5月19日在美國新罕布夏州朴茨茅斯去世。他的墓碑簡單地由一塊普通的石頭做成，上面僅刻着他的姓氏：霍桑。

作品分析

　　美國人民基礎上是以清教價值立國。1620年，這批來自英國的清教徒，因見清除英國國教中天主教殘餘制度無望，乃搭乘「五月花號」（Mayflower），移民北美麻塞諸塞，希望建立一純粹基督徒社會的「新耶路撒冷」，從此被奉為美國最早祖先。

　　由於霍桑生長於清教徒的家庭，清教主義傳統對他影響很深，這種思想滲透到他的作品中，使他一方面擺脫不掉「原罪」、「贖罪」、「內省」和「命定」之類的清教教義，但又從家族的負罪感出發，反過來對清教的專制統治痛心疾首。因此，一方面他反抗這個傳統，抨擊清教狹隘、虛偽的教條；另一方面他又受這個傳統的束縛，以清教的善惡觀念來認識社會和整個世界，這也是他大部作品中滲透着「人本」和「原罪」的對立觀。霍桑的短篇小說《年輕的布朗大爺》正是揭露清教的虛偽，人人皆有的隱祕的罪惡，表達了人性是善與惡交纏的矛盾觀點，特別是其中有許多象徵的意涵，點出象徵技巧在文學作品的運用及重要性，被視為霍桑最佳典型的短篇小說。

　　故事敘及青年善士布朗在某日落時分，告別取名「信仰」（Faith）的妻子，離開所住的村莊，步入黑暗的森林中，途中遇見一帶著「蛇杖」（snake staff），象徵撒旦的旅人，不斷誘惑他參與一場魔鬼的聚會，所經歷一夜個人內心善與惡的交戰。文中的布朗基本就是霍桑本人的心境寫照，魔鬼撒旦在誘惑布朗時，其中，談到如何協助他祖父在「獵巫」運動中，虐殺桂格教派女子及燒殺印地安人，反射霍桑最引以為疚的個人家族歷史，布朗起先靠著「上天與妻子信仰」的支持下，抵抗邪惡對善的引誘：

"With heaven above and Faith below, I will yet stand firm against the devil!" cried Goodman Brown.

但當布朗發現全村的要人，包括他幼時讀經班老師，視同「精神與道德的導師」Goody Closse太太也赴會，最終，連妻子「信仰」竟也參與了魔鬼信徒的聚會，導致他信仰的崩潰，可見「如今世界已無善，只剩邪惡」：

"My Faith is gone!" cried he, after one stupefied moment. "There is no good on earth; and sin is but a name. Come, devil; for to thee is this world given."

布朗走入黑暗又深不可測森林之旅的象徵意義，代表著其內心趨向罪惡的本質，雖然他在緊要關頭抗拒了撒旦的誘惑，但在第二天回到村莊後，這像夢境一般的魔鬼邪教聚會的遭遇，使布朗心靈卻再也沒有恢復平靜，他開始迴避妻子「信仰」，且不時想起那夜在森林中的魔鬼頌歌，最後抑鬱而終。至於小說看完後的兩大疑問：這到底是一場夢境？妻子「信仰」最後是否抵抗了魔鬼的誘惑？反都不具太大意義。

Young Goodman Brown

by Nathaniel Hawthorne

Young Goodman Brown came forth at sunset into the street at Salem village; but put his head back, after crossing the threshold, to exchange a parting kiss with his young wife. And Faith, as the wife was aptly named, thrust her own pretty head into the street, letting the wind play with the pink ribbons of her cap while she called to Goodman Brown.

"Dearest heart," whispered she, softly and rather sadly, when her lips were close to his ear, "prithee (please) put off your journey until sunrise and sleep in your own bed to-night. A lone woman is troubled with such dreams and such thoughts that she's afeard of herself sometimes. Pray tarry with me this night, dear husband, of all nights in the year."

"My love and my Faith," replied young Goodman Brown, "of all nights in the year, this one night must I tarry away from thee. My journey must needs be done 'twixt (between) now and sunrise.

So they parted; and the young man pursued his way until, he looked back and saw the head of Faith still peeping after him with a melancholy air, in spite of her pink ribbons.

With this excellent resolve for the future, Goodman Brown felt himself justified in making more haste on his present evil purpose. He had taken a dreary road, darkened by all the gloomiest trees of the forest, which barely stood aside to let the narrow path creep through, and closed immediately behind. It was all as lonely as could be; and there is this peculiarity in such a solitude…

"There may be a devilish Indian behind every tree," said Goodman Brown to himself; and he glanced fearfully behind him as he added, "What if the devil himself should be at my very elbow!"

His head being turned back, he passed a crook of the road, and, looking forward again, beheld the figure of a man, in grave and decent attire, seated at the foot of an old tree. He arose at Goodman Brown's approach and walked onward side by side with him.

"You are late, Goodman Brown," said he.

"Faith kept me back a while," replied the young man, with a tremor in his voice, caused by the sudden appearance of his companion, though not wholly unexpected.

It was now deep dusk in the forest, and deepest in that part of it where these two were journeying. As nearly as could be discerned, the second traveler was about fifty years old, apparently in the same rank of life as Goodman Brown, and bearing a considerable resemblance to him, though perhaps more in expression than features. Still they might have been taken for father and son. And yet, though the elder person was as simply clad as the younger, and as simple in manner too. But the only thing about him that could be fixed upon as remarkable was his staff, which bore the likeness of a great black snake, so curiously wrought that it might almost be seen to twist and wriggle itself like a living serpent.

"Come, Goodman Brown," cried his fellow-traveler, "this is a dull pace for the beginning of a journey. Take my staff, if you are so soon weary."

"Too far! too far!" exclaimed the goodman, unconsciously resuming his walk. "My father never went into the woods on such an errand, nor his father before him. We have been a race of honest men and good Christians since the days of the martyrs; and shall I be the first of the name of Brown that ever took this path and kept"

"Such company, thou wouldst (you would) say," observed the elder person, interpreting his pause. "Well said, Goodman Brown! I have been as well acquainted with your family as with ever a one among the Puritans; and that's no trifle to say. I helped your grandfather, the constable, when he lashed the Quaker woman so smartly through the streets of Salem; and it was I that brought your father a pitch-pine knot, kindled at my own hearth, to set fire to an Indian village, in King Philip's war. They were my good friends, both; and many a pleasant walk have we had along this path, and returned merrily after midnight. I would fain be friends with you for their sake."

"If it be as thou sayest (you say)," replied Goodman Brown, "I marvel they never spoke of these matters; or, verily, I marvel not, seeing that the least rumor of the sort would have driven them from New England. We are a people of prayer, and good works to boot, and abide no such wickedness."

Thus far the elder traveler had listened with due gravity; but now burst into a fit of irrepressible mirth, shaking himself so violently that his snake-like staff actually seemed to wriggle in sympathy.

"Ha! ha! ha!" shouted he again and again; then composing himself, "Well, go on, Goodman Brown, go on; but, prithee, don't kill me with laughing."

"Well, then, to end the matter at once," said Goodman Brown, considerably nettled, "there is my wife, Faith. It would break her dear little heart; and I'd rather break my own."

"Nay, if that be the case," answered the other, "e'en go thy ways, Goodman Brown. I would not for twenty old women like the one hobbling before us that Faith should come to any harm."

As he spoke he pointed his staff at a female figure on the path, in whom Goodman Brown recognized a very pious and exemplary dame, who had taught him his catechism in youth, and was still his moral and spiritual adviser, jointly with the minister and Deacon Gookin.

…She, meanwhile, was making the best of her way, with singular speed for so aged a woman, and mumbling some indistinct words--a prayer, doubtless--as she went. The traveler put forth his staff and touched her withered neck with what seemed the serpent's tail.

"The devil!" screamed the pious old lady…"So, being all ready for the meeting, and no horse to ride on, I made up my mind to foot it; for they tell me there is a nice young man to be taken into communion to-night. But now your good worship will lend me your arm, and we shall be there in a twinkling."

"That can hardly be," answered her friend. "I may not spare you my arm, Goody Cloyse; but here is my staff, if you will."

So saying, he threw it down at her feet, where, perhaps, it assumed life, being one of the rods which its owner had formerly lent to the Egyptian magi. Of this fact, however, Goodman Brown could not take cognizance. He had cast up his eyes in astonishment, and, looking down again, beheld neither Goody Cloyse nor the serpentine staff, but his fellow-traveler alone, who waited for him as calmly as if nothing had happened.

"That old woman taught me my catechism," said Goodman Brown; and there was a world of meaning in this simple comment.

They continued to walk onward, while the elder traveler exhorted his companion to make good speed and persevere in the path, discoursing so aptly that his arguments seemed rather to spring up in the bosom of his auditor than to be suggested by himself. As they went, he plucked a branch of maple to serve for a walking stick, and began to strip it of the twigs and little boughs, which were wet with evening dew. The moment his fingers touched them they became strangely withered and dried up as with a week's sunshine. Thus the pair proceeded, at a good free pace, until suddenly, in a gloomy hollow of the road, Goodman Brown sat himself down on the stump of a tree and refused to go any farther.

"Friend," said he, stubbornly, "my mind is made up. Not another step will I budge on this errand. What if a wretched old woman do choose to go to the devil when I thought she was going to heaven: is that any reason why I should quit my dear Faith and go after her?"

"You will think better of this by and by," said his acquaintance, composedly. "Sit here and rest yourself a while; and when you feel like moving again, there is my staff to help you along."

Without more words, he threw his companion the maple stick, and was as speedily out of sight as if he had vanished into the deepening gloom. The young man sat a few moments by the roadside, applauding himself greatly, and thinking with how clear a conscience he should meet the minister in his morning walk, nor shrink from the eye of good old Deacon Gookin. And what calm sleep would be his that very night, which was to have been spent so wickedly, but so purely and sweetly now, in the arms of Faith! Amidst these pleasant and praiseworthy meditations, Goodman Brown heard the tramp of horses along the road, …, that he recognized the voices of the minister and Deacon Gookin, jogging along quietly, ...

"Of the two, reverend sir," said the voice like the deacon's, "I had rather miss an ordination dinner than to-night's meeting. They tell me that some of our community are to be here from Falmouth and beyond, and others from Connecticut and Rhode Island, besides several of the Indian powwows, who, after their fashion, know almost as much deviltry as the best of us. Moreover, there is a goodly young woman to be taken into communion."

Young Goodman Brown caught hold of a tree for support, being ready to sink down on the ground, faint and overburdened with the heavy sickness of his heart. He looked up to the sky, doubting whether there really was a heaven above him. Yet there was the blue arch, and the stars brightening in it.

"With heaven above and Faith below, I will yet stand firm against the devil!" cried Goodman Brown.

…The next moment, so indistinct were the sounds, he doubted whether he had heard aught but the murmur of the old forest, whispering without a wind. Then came a stronger swell of those familiar tones, heard daily in the sunshine at Salem village, but never until now from a cloud of night. There was one voice of a young woman, uttering lamentations, yet with an uncertain sorrow, and entreating for some favor, which, perhaps, it would grieve her to obtain; and all the unseen multitude, both saints and sinners, seemed to encourage her onward.

"Faith!" shouted Goodman Brown, in a voice of agony and desperation; and the echoes of the forest mocked him, crying, "Faith! Faith!" as if bewildered wretches were seeking her all through the wilderness.

And, maddened with despair, so that he laughed loud and long, did Goodman Brown grasp his staff and set forth again, at such a rate that he seemed to fly along the forest path rather than to walk or run. The road grew wilder and drearier and more faintly traced, and vanished at length, leaving him in the heart of the dark wilderness, still rushing onward with the instinct that guides mortal man to evil.

Thus sped the demoniac on his course, until, quivering among the trees, he saw a red light before him, as when the felled trunks and branches of a clearing have been set on fire, and throw up their lurid blaze against the sky, at the hour of midnight. He paused, in a lull of the tempest that had driven him onward, and heard the swell of what seemed a hymn, rolling solemnly from a distance with the weight of many voices. He knew the tune; it was a familiar one in the choir of the village meeting-house.

In the interval of silence he stole forward until the light glared full upon his eyes. At one extremity of an open space, hemmed in by the dark wall of the forest, arose a rock, bearing some rude, natural resemblance either to an alter or a pulpit, and surrounded by four blazing pines, their tops aflame, their stems untouched, like candles at an evening meeting. The mass of foliage that had overgrown the summit of the rock was all on fire, blazing high into the night and fitfully illuminating the whole field.

*

"Bring forth the converts!" cried a voice that echoed through the field and rolled into the forest.

At the word, Goodman Brown stepped forth from the shadow of the trees and approached the congregation, with whom he felt a loathful brotherhood by the sympathy of all that was wicked in his heart. He could have well-nigh sworn that the shape of his own dead father beckoned him to advance, looking downward from a smoke wreath, while a woman, with dim features of despair, threw out her hand to warn him back. Was it his mother? But he had no power to retreat one step, nor to resist, even in thought, when the minister and good old Deacon Gookin seized his arms and led him to the blazing rock. Thither came also the slender form of a veiled female, led between Goody Cloyse, that pious teacher of the catechism, and Martha Carrier, who had received the devil's promise to be queen of hell. A rampant hag was she. And there stood the proselytes beneath the canopy of fire.

"Welcome, my children," said the dark figure, "to the communion of your race. Ye (you) have found thus young your nature and your destiny. My children, look behind you!"

They turned; and flashing forth, as it were, in a sheet of flame, the fiend worshippers were seen; the smile of welcome gleamed darkly on every visage.

"There," resumed the sable form, "are all whom ye have reverenced from youth. Ye deemed them holier than yourselves, and shrank from your own sin, contrasting it with their lives of righteousness and prayerful aspirations heavenward. Yet here are they all in my worshipping assembly. Far more than this. It shall be yours to penetrate, in every bosom, the deep mystery of sin, the fountain of all wicked arts, and which inexhaustibly supplies more evil impulses than human power--than my power at its utmost--can make manifest in deeds. And now, my children, look upon each other."

They did so; and, by the blaze of the hell-kindled torches, the wretched man beheld his Faith, and the wife her husband, trembling before that unhallowed altar.

"Lo, there ye stand, my children," said the figure, in a deep and solemn tone, almost sad with its despairing awfulness, as if his once angelic nature could yet mourn for our miserable race. "Depending upon one another's hearts, ye had still hoped that virtue were not all a dream. Now are ye undeceived. Evil is the nature of mankind. Evil must be your only happiness. Welcome again, my children, to the communion of your race."

"Welcome," repeated the fiend worshippers, in one cry of despair and triumph.

And there they stood, the only pair, as it seemed, who were yet hesitating on the verge of wickedness in this dark world. A basin was hollowed, naturally, in the rock. Did it contain water? or was it blood? or, perchance, a liquid flame? Herein did the shape of evil dip his hand and prepare to lay the mark of baptism upon their foreheads, that they might be partakers of the mystery of sin, more conscious of the secret guilt of others, both in deed and thought, than they could now be of their own. The husband cast one look at his pale wife, and Faith at him.

"Faith! Faith!" cried the husband, "look up to heaven, and resist the wicked one."

Whether Faith obeyed he knew not. Hardly had he spoken when he found himself amid calm night and solitude, listening to a roar of the wind which died heavily away through the forest. He staggered against the rock, and felt it chill and damp; while a hanging twig, that had been all on fire, besprinkled his cheek with the coldest dew.

The next morning young Goodman Brown came slowly into the street of Salem village, staring around him like a bewildered man. The good old minister was taking a walk along the graveyard to get an appetite for breakfast and meditate his sermon, and bestowed a blessing, as he passed, on Goodman Brown. He shrank from the venerable saint as if to avoid an anathema. Old Deacon Gookin was at domestic worship, and the holy words of his prayer were heard through the open window. "What God doth the wizard pray to?" quoth Goodman Brown. Goody Cloyse, that excellent old Christian, stood in the early sunshine at her own lattice, catechizing a little girl who had brought her a pint of morning's milk. Goodman Brown snatched away the child as from the grasp of the fiend himself. Turning the corner by the meeting-house, he spied the head of Faith, with the pink ribbons, gazing anxiously forth, and bursting into such joy at sight of him that she skipped along the street and almost kissed her husband before the whole village. But Goodman Brown looked sternly and sadly into her face, and passed on without a greeting.

Had Goodman Brown fallen asleep in the forest and only dreamed a wild dream of a witch-meeting?

On the Sabbath day, when the congregation were singing a holy psalm, he could not listen because an anthem of sin rushed loudly upon his ear and drowned all the blessed strain. When the minister spoke from the pulpit with power and fervid eloquence, and, with his hand on the open

Bible, of the sacred truths of our religion, then did Goodman Brown turn pale. Often, waking suddenly at midnight, he shrank from the bosom of Faith; and at morning or eventide, when the family knelt down at prayer, he scowled and muttered to himself, and gazed sternly at his wife, and turned away. And when he had lived long, and was borne to his grave a hoary corpse, followed by Faith, an aged woman, and children and grandchildren, a goodly procession, besides neighbors not a few, they carved no hopeful verse upon his tombstone, for his dying hour was gloom.

3 愛倫‧坡《弗德馬先生案的真相》
——黑色浪漫之娛樂泰斗

小說特徵

驚悚、懸疑之「黑色浪漫主義」
（Dark Romanticism）

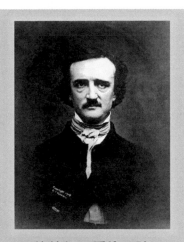

埃德加‧愛倫‧玻
（Edgar Allan Poe, 1809-1849）

Words have no power to impress the mind without the exquisite horror. I have no faith in human perfectability. Man is now not more happy--nor more wise, than he was 6000 years ago.

-Edgar Allan Poe

文字沒有強烈恐懼，就沒有深印人心的力量。我對人性的完美沒有信心。比起六千年前，人是既沒更快樂，也沒更具智慧。

——愛倫‧坡

作者短評

　　埃德加・愛倫・坡（Edgar Allan Poe），1809年，生於美國麻薩諸塞州波士頓，愛倫・坡主要為其養父約翰愛倫（John Allan）所撫養長大，而將「愛倫」冠入其中間名（middle name），妻逝後，酗酒，生活潦倒，1849年10月7日，愛倫・坡倒臥巴爾的摩溝壑之中，死因不明，得年四十歲。

　　愛倫・坡在他短暫四十歲生命中，思想鎖定人性陰暗面，視人生乃痛苦與恐懼之源，擅長描寫異想人格、犯罪心理、志怪、奇幻這類的題材，探討人類心靈最深層的陰鬱，其中小說情節設計和鋪陳技巧，引人入勝，創造晦暗、恐怖、詭祕的氛圍，作品滿布哀傷鬼魅。

　　愛倫・坡作品結構上之特色與元素，喜好以死亡和恐懼為主題，除謀殺，鬼魅、怪異的劇情，想像不拘，具有高度驚異、創新特色之效果，為市場暢銷之保證。《莫爾格街兇殺案》（*The Murders in the Rue Morgue, 1841*），不但被公認為史上的第一本推理小說，同時也上演了史上的第一宗密室殺人詭計（locked room mystery）。書中神探杜平（C. Auguste Dupin），也被當成小說世界裡的第一位神探，成為許多後起仿傚的典範，最出名者莫過於日後之英國神探福爾摩斯，所用第一人稱敘述案情，娓娓道來時的臨場感，根本是愛倫・坡之翻版。愛倫・坡總能帶領讀者進入人性最深的恐懼之中，作品影響文壇甚遠，奉為經典，歷久不衰，在美國文壇獨樹一格的地位，和當時大盛於美國，由艾默生、梭羅等領銜之本土文學理論——「超越文學」（Transcendentalism），強調人性「止於至善」光明面的浪漫文風，大異其趣。

另外，愛倫‧坡在十九世紀人類科技萌芽時期，雖然沒有那麼多相關作品可以參考，他卻勇於走在時代的尖端，大量放入科幻的想像，連今日的《阿凡達》導演詹姆士柯麥隆與史蒂芬史匹柏，亦望塵莫及，益增他作品可讀性的優勢。

作品分析

常有人問：「一個好的小說標準在那裡？」，答案見仁見智，莫衷一是；然排除個人喜好的主觀因素，或許我們可以求助於米蘭昆德拉在〈小說的藝術〉中，提供之「小說的四個召喚」，不失為評論小說的一個客觀軟體：

（一）遊戲的召喚：趣味、娛樂性。

（二）夢的召喚：創意、創新性。

（三）思想的召喚：深度、深刻性。

（四）時間的召喚：感動、感人力量。

也就是說小說的高下，除繼承文學上，貼近真實人生，表現創意、深度與藝術價值外，大眾市場的娛樂性，也是重要的評量標準。至少，就最後一標準言，愛倫‧坡結合驚悚與懸疑，所創作黑色浪漫小說，極具取悅大眾，高度趣味價值，幫助他被公認是推理、偵探小說之父，甚至被視為科幻小說催生者。

在《弗德馬先生案的真相》小說中，我們可以輕鬆的看出，它包含了所有愛倫‧坡創作想像的元素，主角是一名催眠師，希望運用催眠術於阻止死亡，而身患肺結核，來日無多的弗德馬先生甘願成為主角的實驗對象，待弗德馬先生死前一刻，主角開始向他施行了催眠，弗德馬先生也果然在催眠狀態下身體進入死亡狀態，但恐怖是，他卻能活著告訴催眠者自己已經死了，充滿了驚恐與異想的氣氛：

"Yes;--no;--I *have been* sleeping--and now--now--*I am dead*."

弗德馬先生這種不生不死的狀態持了十個月，弗德馬先生看來也是不好受，終於接受喚醒的要求：

"For God's sake!--quick!--quick!--put me to sleep--or, quick!--waken me!--quick!--*I say to you that I am dead!*"

主角終於向弗德馬先生解除催眠，弗德馬先生立即發為一灘臭水。可說是非常典型的愛倫‧坡式的集科幻、想像與鬼魅於大成的小說風格作品。

The Facts In The Case of M. Valdemar

by Edgar Allan Poe

My attention, for the last three years, had been repeatedly drawn to the subject of Mesmerism; and, about nine month ago, it occurred to me, quite suddenly, that in the series of experiments made hitherto, there had been a very remarkable and most unaccountable omission:--no person had as yet been mesmerized *in articulo mortis*. It remained to be seen, to what extend, or *for how long a period, the encroachments of Death might be arrested by the process.*

When the ideas to which I have alluded first occurred to me, it was of course very natural that I should think of M. Valdemar. I knew he had no relatives in America who would be likely to interfere. I spoke to him frankly upon the subject; and to my surprise, his interest seemed vividly excited. His disease was of that character which would admit of exact calculation in respect to the epoch of its termination in death; and it was finally arranged between us that he would send for me about twenty-four hours before the period announced by his physicians as that of his decease.

It is now rather more than seven months since I received, from M. Valdemar himself, the subjoined note:

MY DEAR P--

You may as well come *now*. D-- and F-- are agreed that I cannot hold out beyond to-morrow midnight; and I think they have hit the time very nearly.

VALDEMAR.

I received this note within half an hour after it was written, and in fifteen minutes more I was in the dying man's chamber. I had not seen him for ten days, and was appalled by the fearful alteration which the brief interval had wrought in him. His face wore a leaden hue; the eyes were utterly lustreless; and the emaciation was so extreme, that the skin had been broken through by the cheek-bones. His expectoration was excessive. The pulse was barely perceptible. He was propped up in the bed by pillows. Doctors D-- and F-- were in attendance... I took these gentlemen aside, and obtained from them a minute account of the patient's condition. It was the opinion of both physicians that M. Valdemar would die about midnight on the morrow (Sunday.) It was then seven o'clock on Saturday evening.

I spoke freely with M. Valdemar on the subject of the experiment proposed. He still professed himself quite willing and even anxious to have it made, and urged me to commence it at once. A male and a female nurse were in attendance; but I did not feel myself altogether at liberty to engage in a task of this character with no more reliable witnesses than these people, in case of sudden accident, might prove.

When... it was fully midnight, and I requested the gentlemen present to examine M. Valdemar's condition. After a few experiments, they admitted him to be in a perfect state of mesmeric trance...We left M. Valdemar entirely undisturbed until about three o'clock in the morning, when I approached him and found him in precisely the same condition-the pulse was imperceptible; the breathing was gentle; the eyes were closed naturally; and the limbs were as rigid and as cold as marble. Still, the general appearance was not that of death.

In such experiments with this patient, I had never perfectly succeeded before, and assuredly I had little thought of succeeding now; but to my astonishment, his arm very readily, although feebly, followed every direction I assigned it with mine. I determined to hazard a few words of conversation.

"M. Valdemar," I said, "are you asleep?" He made no answer, but I perceived a tremor about the lips, and was thus induced to repeat the question, again and again. At its third repetition, his whole frame was agitated by a very slight shivering; the eyelids unclosed themselves so far as to display a white line of a ball; the lips moved sluggishly, and from between them, in a barely audible whisper, issued the words:

"Yes;--asleep now. Do not wake me!--let me die so!"

Here I felt the limbs, and found them as rigid as ever. The right arm, as before, obeyed the direction of my hand. I questioned the sleep-waker again:

"Do you still feel pain in the breast, M. Valdemar?"

The answer now was immediate, but even less audible than before:

"No pain--I am dying!"

I did not think it advisable to disturb him further just then, and nothing more was said or done until the arrival of Dr. F--, who came a little before sunrise, and expressed unbounded astonishment at finding the patient still alive. After feeling the pulse and applying a mirror to the lips, he requested me to speak to the sleep-waker again. I did so, saying:

"M. Valdemar, do you still sleep?"

As before, some minutes elapsed; and during the interval the dying man seemed to be collecting his energies to speak. At my fourth repetition of the question, he said very faintly, almost inaudibly:

"Yes; still asleep--dying."

It was now the opinion, or rather the wish, of the physicians, that M. Valdemar should be suffered to remain undisturbed in his present apparently tranquil condition, until death should supervene--and this, it was generally agreed, must now take place within a few minutes. I concluded, however, to speak to him once more, and merely repeated my previous question.

While I spoke, there came a marked change over the countenance of the sleep-waker. The eyes rolled themselves slowly open, the pupils disappearing upwardly; the skin generally assumed a cadaverous hue, resembling not so much parchment as white paper; and the circular hectic spots which, hitherto, had been strongly defined in the centre of each cheek, *went out* at once. I use this expression, because the suddenness of their departure put me in mind of nothing so much as the extinguishment of a candle by a puff of the breath. The upper lip, at the same time, writhed itself away from the teeth, which it had previously covered completely; while the lower jaw fell with an audible jerk, leaving the mouth widely extended, and disclosing in full view the swollen and blackened tongue. I presume that no member of the party then present had been unaccustomed to death-bed horrors; but so hideous beyond conception was the appearance of M. Valdemar at this moment, that there was a general shrinking back from the region of the bed.

I now feel that I have reached a point of this narrative at which every reader will be startled into positive disbelief. It is my business, however, simply to proceed.

There was no longer the faintest sign of vitality in M. Valdemar; and concluding him to be dead, we were consigning him to the charge of the nurses, when a strong vibratory motion was observable in the tongue. This continued for perhaps a minute. At the expiration of this period, there issued from the distended and motionless jaws a voice- such as it would be madness in me to attempt describing.

M. Valdemar *spoke*--obviously in reply to the question I had propounded to him a few minutes before. I had asked him, it will be remembered, if he still slept. Now he said:

"Yes; --no; --I *have been* sleeping --and now –now --*I am dead*."

No person present even affected to deny, or attempted to repress, the unutterable, shuddering horror which these few words, thus uttered, were so well calculated to convey. Mr. L-- (the student) swooned. The nurses immediately left the chamber, and could not be induced to return. My own impressions I would not pretend to render intelligible to the reader. For nearly an hour, we busied ourselves, silently--without the utterance of a word--in endeavors to revive Mr. L--l. When he came to himself, we addressed ourselves again to an investigation of M. Valdemar's condition.

The only real indication, indeed, of the mesmeric influence, was now found in the vibratory movement of the tongue, whenever I addressed M. Valdemar a question. He seemed to be making an effort to reply, but had no longer sufficient volition. To queries put to him by any other person than myself he seemed utterly insensible--although I endeavored to place each member of the company in mesmeric *rapport* with him. I believe that I have now related all that is necessary to an understanding of the sleep-waker's state at this epoch. Other nurses were procured; and at ten o'clock I left the house in company with the two physicians and Mr. L--l.

In the afternoon we all called again to see the patient. His condition remained precisely the same. We had now some discussion as to the propriety and feasibility of awakening him; but we had little difficulty in agreeing that no good purpose would be served by so doing. It seemed clear to us all that to awaken M. Valdemar would be merely to insure his instant, or at least his speedy, dissolution.

From this period until the close of last week--*an interval of nearly seven months*--we continued to make daily calls at M. Valdemar's house, accompanied, now and then, by medical and other friends. All this time the sleep-waker remained *exactly* as I have last described him. The nurses' attentions were continual.

It was on Friday last that we finally resolved to make the experiment of awakening, or attempting to awaken him.

For the purpose of relieving M. Valdemar from the mesmeric trance, I made use of the customary passes. These for a time were unsuccessful.

It was now suggested that I should attempt to influence the patient's arm as heretofore. I made the attempt and failed. Dr. F-- then intimated a desire to have me put a question. I did so, as follows:

"M. Valdemar, can you explain to us what are your feelings or wishes now?"

There was an instant return of the hectic circles on the cheeks: the tongue quivered, or rather rolled violently in the mouth (although the jaws and lips remained rigid as before), and at length the same hideous voice which I have already described, broke forth:

"For God's sake!--quick!--quick!--put me to sleep--or, quick!--waken me!--quick!--*I say to you that I am dead!*"

I was thoroughly unnerved, and for an instant remained undecided what to do. At first I made an endeavor to recompose the patient; but, failing in this through total abeyance of the will, I retraced my steps and as earnestly struggled to awaken him. In this attempt I soon saw that I should be successful--or at least I soon fancied that my success would be complete--and I am sure that all in the room were prepared to see the patient awaken. For what really occurred, however, it is quite impossible that any human being could have been prepared.

As I rapidly made the mesmeric passes, amid ejaculations of "dead! dead!" absolutely *bursting* from the tongue and not from the lips of the sufferer, his whole frame at once--within the space of a single minute, or less, shrunk -- crumbled--absolutely *rotted* away beneath my hands. Upon the bed, before the whole company, there lay a nearly liquid mass of loathsome--of detestable putrescence.

赫爾曼‧梅爾維爾《提琴手》
——人性中的宿命式悲劇

小說特徵

人性宿命、清教、象徵主義

赫爾曼‧梅爾維爾
（Herman Melville, 1819-1891）

With genius and without fame, he is happier than a king.
-Herman Melville

一個沒有榮耀的天才，他比國王更快樂。

——赫爾曼‧梅爾維爾

作者短評

　　赫爾曼・梅爾維爾（Herman Melville），1819年，出生於紐約。十三歲時，父親經商失敗破產，留下一家九口，於是梅爾維爾自十五歲，就輟學開始外出工作。1839年起，梅爾維爾成為捕鯨船水手，航行於南太平洋一帶，曾在南太平洋馬克薩斯群島被提比（Typee）食人族所俘虜，脫逃後，1846年，他根據這一經歷，發表《提比》（Typee）小說，隔年又發表《渥姆》（Omoo）也是《提比》的續集。

　　1850年，他以其海上捕鯨的經歷為事實，開始創作《白鯨記》（Moby Dick），前後花了17個月，1851年夏完稿，同年出版。梅爾維爾《白鯨記》這部小說日後被認為是美國最偉大的小說之一，但第一年竟然只賣出5本，在當時非但沒有引起轟動，並惹來許多的非議，使他十分失望，梅爾維爾生前默默無聞，晚年轉而寫詩，出版商拒絕繼續讓他預支稿費，他曾寫信給霍桑：「激動我的心靈，促使我寫作的東西，我寫不成了——因為它無利可圖。可是要我改弦更張，不這麼寫，我辦不到。」1891年9月28日，梅爾維爾過世於紐約，窮途潦倒以終。

　　《白鯨記》直到出版後七十年，才獲得重視。英國作家毛姆在《世界十大小說家及其代表作》一書中對《白鯨記》的評價遠在美國其他作家愛倫・坡與馬克・吐溫之上。

作品分析

就大部份超越主義（美國版之浪漫文學）作家作品觀察，都是對個人精神及品性，作光明面的推揚；人性本善，所以個人的理性判斷總是成功、美滿，個人的選擇，也往往是以喜劇結局。但超越主義作家中，也不乏對人性力量做反面悲觀思考的創作，形成美國浪漫文學藝術中另股主流。最出名除霍桑外，梅爾維爾則屬另一代表。兩人代表之作《紅字》與《白鯨記》中，兩書的主角：無論是牧師丁斯戴爾（Dismsdale）或阿巴（Ahab）船長都無法抗拒清教與白鯨的吞噬，暗喻人性中不可改變的宿命式悲劇。

在小說寫作上，梅爾維爾深受莎士比亞與霍桑的啟發與影響最大，一心以兩人為效法對象，梅爾維爾認為莎士比亞之所以能為莎士比亞，乃在於他能刻畫生活的醜惡面，而梅爾維爾視霍桑是最好的朋友，也在他發現霍桑的作品中，具有莎士比亞一樣的特質，曾說：「吸引我並使我入迷的是霍桑作品中所表現的醜陋面。」，梅爾維爾深愛霍桑的小說《紅字》。同樣，當梅爾維爾1850年2月，埋首《白鯨記》的寫作時，梅爾維爾寫信給霍桑說：「我寫了一本邪書，不過，我覺得像羔羊一般潔白無疵」，霍桑手邊曾有一本梅爾維爾致贈的《白鯨記》，梅爾維爾和霍桑的創作皆帶有宗教神秘和悲觀的色彩，霍桑深受清教的影響，梅爾維爾喜讀聖經，他《白鯨記》即受來自聖經中約拿（Jonah）拒絕接受上帝召喚前往與以色列為敵的尼尼微城（Nineveh）宣教，企圖坐船逃跑，而被上帝所派的鯨魚吞到肚中的啟發，梅爾維爾也效法霍桑，喜好象徵手法的運用，書中的白鯨宛如自然界無法抗拒的力量，有如人生命運的譬喻，船長阿巴的「註定失敗，仍要奮鬥」的追捕白鯨，最後卻反為白鯨所噬，充滿叛逆英雄的悲劇性，暗喻個人自我實現的堅持，不只是個人的解放，也會是自我毀滅。

　　本書所選梅爾維爾的短篇小說《提琴手》，全文簡潔明快，藉著一位沒有天份卻汲營於虛名的悲憤作家，和一位具有天份卻又放棄一切名利而滿足自在提琴家的故事，告訴人有沒有天賦或名氣不是決定你人生滿意與否的主因，個人的快樂跟他們是沒有太大的關係，人生其實是有捨才有得，放手反而才能擁有。

文選閱讀

The Fiddler

by Herman Melville

So my poem is damned, and immortal fame is not for me! I am nobody forever and ever. Intolerable fate?

Snatching my hat, I dashed down the criticism, and rushed out into Broadway, where enthusiastic throngs were crowding to a circus in a side-street near by, very recently started, and famous for a capital clown.

Presently my old friend Standard rather boisterously accosted me.

"Well met, Helmstone, my boy! Ah! what's the matter? Haven't been committing murder? Ain't flying justice? You look wild!"

"You have seen it then?" said I, of course referring to the critism.

"Oh yes; I was there at the morning performance. Great clown, I assure you. But here comes Hautboy. Hautboy-Helmstone."

Without having time or inclination to resent so mortifying a mistake, I was instantly soothed as I gazed on the face of the new acquaintance so unceremoniously introduced. His person was short and full, with a juvenile, animated cast to it. His complexion rurally ruddy; his eye sincere, cheery, and gray. His hair alone betrayed that he was not an overgrown boy. From his hair I set him down as forty or more.

"Come, Standard," he gleefully cried to my friend, "are you not going to the circus? The clown is inimitable, they say. Come; Mr. Helmstone, too--come both; and circus over, we'll take a nice stew and punch at Taylor's."

The sterling content, good humor, and extraordinary ruddy, sincere expression of this most singular new acquaintance acted upon me like magic. It seemed mere loyalty to human nature to accept an invitation from so unmistakably kind and honest a heart.

The sterling content, good humor, and extraordinary ruddy, sincere expression of this most singular new acquaintance acted upon me like magic. It seemed mere loyalty to human nature to accept an invitation from so unmistakably kind and honest a heart.

During the circus performance I kept my eye more on Hautboy than on the celebrated clown. Hautboy was the sight for me. Such genuine enjoyment as his struck me to the soul with a sense of the reality of the thing called happiness. The jokes of the clown he seemed to roll under his tongue as ripe magnum bonums. Now the foot, now the hand, was employed to attest his grateful applause. At any hit more than ordinary, he turned upon Standard and me to see if his rare pleasure was shared. In a man of forty I saw a boy of twelve; and this too without the slightest abatement of my respect. Because all was so honest and natural, every expression and attitude so graceful with genuine good-nature, that the marvelous juvenility of Hautboy assumed a sort of divine and immortal air, like that of some forever youthful god of Greece.

But much as I gazed upon Hautboy, and as much as I admired his air, yet that desperate mood in which I had first rushed from the house had not so entirely departed as not to molest me with momentary returns. But from these relapses I would rouse myself, and swiftly glance round the broad amphitheatre of eagerly interested and all-applauding human faces. Hark! claps, thumps, deafening huzzas; the vast assembly seemed frantic, with acclamation; and what, mused I, has caused all this? Why, the clown only comically grinned with one of his extra grins.

Then I repeated in my mind that sublime passage in my poem, in which Cleothemes the Argive vindicates the justice of the war. Aye, aye, thought I to myself, did I now leap into the ring there, and repeat that identical passage, nay, enact the whole tragic poem before them, would they applaud the poet as they applaud the clown? No! They would hoot me, and call me doting or mad. Then what does this prove? Your infatuation or their insensibility? Perhaps both; but indubitably the first. But why wail? Do you seek admiration from the admirers of a buffoon? Call to mind the saying of the Athenian, who when the people vociferously applauded in the forum, asked his friend in a whisper, what foolish thing had he said?

Again my eye swept the circus, and fell on the ruddy radiance of the countenance of Hautboy. But its clear honest cheeriness disdained my disdain. My intolerant pride was rebuked. And yet Hautboy dreamed not what magic reproof to a soul like mine sat on his laughing brow. At the very instant I felt the dart of the censure, his eye twinkled, his hand waved, his voice was lifted in jubilant delight at another joke of the inexhaustible clown.

Circus over, we went to Taylor's. Among crowds of others, we sat down to our stews and punches at one of the small marble tables. Hautboy sat opposite to me. Though greatly subdued from its former hilarity, his face still shone with gladness. But added to this was a quality not so prominent before: a certain serene expression of leisurely, deep good sense. Good sense and good humor in him joined hands. As the conversation proceeded between the brisk Standard and him--for I said little or nothing--I was more and more struck with the excellent judgment he evinced. In most of his remarks upon a variety of topics Hautboy seemed intuitively to hit the exact line between enthusiasm and apathy. It was plain that while Hautboy saw the world pretty much as it was, yet he did not theoretically espouse its bright side nor its dark side. Rejecting all solutions, he but acknowledged facts. What was sad in the world he did not superficially gainsay; what was glad in it he! did not cynically slur; and all which was to him personally enjoyable, he gratefully took to his heart. It was plain, then--so it seemed at that moment, at least--that his extraordinary cheerfulness did not arise either from deficiency of feeling or thought.

Suddenly remembering an engagement, he took up his hat, bowed pleasantly, and left us.

"Well, Helmstone," said Standard, inaudibly drumming on the slab, "what do you think of your new acquaintance?"

The two last words tingled with a peculiar and novel significance.

"New acquaintance indeed," echoed I. "Standard, I owe you a thousand thanks for introducing me to one of the most singular men I have ever seen. It needed the optical sight of such a man to believe in the possibility of his existence."

"You rather like him, then," said Standard, with ironical dryness.

"I hugely love and admire him, Standard. I wish I were Hautboy."

"Ah? That's a pity, now. There's only one Hautboy in the world."

This last remark set me to pondering again, and somehow it revived my dark mood.

"His wonderful cheerfulness, I suppose," said I, sneering with spleen, "originates not less in a felicitous fortune than in a felicitous temper. His great good sense is apparent; but great good sense may exist without sublime endowments. Nay, I take it, in certain cases, that good sense is simply owing to the absence of those. Much more, cheerfulness. Unpossessed of genius, Hautboy is eternally blessed."

"Ah? You would not think him an extraordinary genius, then?"

"Genius? What! such a short, fat fellow a genius! Genius, like Cassius, is lank."

"Ah? But could you not fancy that Hautboy might formerly have had genius, but luckily getting rid of it, at last fatted up?"

"For a genius to get rid of his genius is as impossible as for a man in the galloping consumption to get rid of that."

"Ah? You speak very decidedly."

"Yes, Standard," cried I, increasing in spleen, "your cheery Hautboy, after all, is no pattern, no lesson for you and me. With average abilities; opinions clear, because circumscribed; passions docile, because they are feeble; a temper hilarious, because he was born to it--how can your Hautboy be made a reasonable example to a handy fellow like you, or an ambitious dreamer like me?"

Nothing tempts him beyond common limit; in himself he has nothing to restrain. By constitution he is exempted from all moral harm. Could ambition but prick him; had he but once heard applause, or endured contempt, a very different man would your Hautboy be. Acquiescent and calm from the cradle to the grave, he obviously slides through the crowd.

"Ah?"

"Why do you say Ah to me so strangely whenever I speak?"

"Did you ever hear of Master Betty?"

"The great English prodigy, who long ago ousted the Siddons and the Kembles from Drury Lane, and made the whole town run mad with acclamation?"

"The same," said Standard, once more inaudibly drumming on the slab.

I looked at him perplexed. He seemed to be holding the master-key of our theme in mysterious reserve; seemed to be throwing out his Master Betty, too, to puzzle me only the more.

"What under heaven can Master Betty, the great genius and prodigy, and English boy twelve years old, have to do with the poor commonplace plodder, Hautboy, an American of forty?"

"Oh, nothing in the least. I don't imagine that they ever saw each other. Besides, Master Betty must be dead and buried long ere this."

"Then why cross the ocean, and rifle the grave to drag his remains into this living discussion?"

"Absent-mindedness, I suppose. I humbly beg pardon. Proceed with your observations on Hautboy. You think he never had genius, quite too contented, and happy and fat for that--ah? You think him no pattern for men in general? affording no lesson of value to neglected merit, genius ignored, or impotent presumption rebuked?--all of which three amount to much the same thing. You admire his cheerfulness, while scorning his commonplace soul. Poor Hautboy, how sad that your very cheerfulness should, by a by-blow, bring you despite!"

"I don't say I scorn him; you are unjust. I simply declare that he is no pattern for me."

A sudden noise at my side attracted my ear. Turning, I saw Hautboy again, who very blithely reseated himself on the chair he had left.

"I was behind time with my engagement," said Hautboy, "so thought I would run back and rejoin you. But come, you have sat long enough here. Let us go to my rooms. It is only a five minutes' walk."

"If you will promise to fiddle for us, we will," said Standard.

Fiddle! thought I--he's a jiggumbob fiddler, then? No wonder genius declines to measure its pace to a fiddler's bow. My spleen was very strong on me now.

"I will gladly fiddle you your fill," replied Hautboy to Standard. "Come on."

In a few minutes we found ourselves in the fifth story of a sort of storehouse, in a lateral street to Broadway. It was curiously furnished with all sorts of odd furniture which seemed to have been obtained, piece by piece, at auctions of old-fashioned household stuff. But all was charmingly clean and cozy.

Pressed by Standard, Hautboy forthwith got out his dented old fiddle and, sitting down on a tall rickety stool, played away right merrily at "Yankee Doodle" and other off-handed, dashing, and disdainfully care-free airs. But common as were the tunes, I was transfixed by something miraculously superior in the style. Sitting there on the old stool, his rusty hat sidways cocked on his head, one foot dangling adrift, he plied the bow of an enchanter. All my moody discontent, every vestige of peevishness, fled. My whole splenetic soul capitulated to the magical fiddle.

"Something of an Orpheus, ah?" said Standard, archly nudging me beneath the left rib.

"And I, the charmed Briun," murmured I.

The fiddle ceased. Once more, with redoubled curiosity, I gazed upon the easy, indifferent Hautboy. But he entirely baffled inquisition.

When, leaving him, Standard and I were in the street once more, I earnestly conjured him to tell me who, in sober truth, this marvelous Hautboy was.

"Why, haven't you seen him? And didn't you yourself lay his whole anatomy open on the marble slab at Taylor's? What more can you possibly learn? Doubtless, your own masterly insight has already put you in possession of all."

"You mock me, Standard. There is some mystery here. Tell me, I entreat you, who is Hautboy?"

"An extraordinary genius, Helmstone," said Standard, with sudden ardor, "who in boyhood drained the whole flagon of glory; whose going from city to city was a going from triumph to triumph. One who has been an object of wonder to the wisest, been caressed by the loveliest, received the open homage of thousands on thousands of the rabble. But to-day he walks Broadway and no man knows him. With you and me, the elbow of the hurrying clerk, and the pole of the remorseless omnibus, shove him. He who has a hundred times been crowned with laurels, now wears, as you see, a bunged beaver. Once fortune poured showers of gold into his lap, as showers of laurel leaves upon his brow. To-day, from house to house he hies, teaching fiddling for a living. Crammed once with fame, he is now hilarious without it. With genius and without fame, he is happier than a king. More a prodigy now than ever."

"His true name?"

"Let me whisper it in your ear."

"What! Oh, Standard, myself, as a child, have shouted myself hoarse applauding that very name in the theatre."

"I have heard your poem was not very handsomely received," said Standard, now suddenly shifting the subject.

"Not a word of that, for Heaven's sake!" cried I. "If Cicero, traveling in the East, found sympathetic solace for his grief in beholding the arid overthrow of a once gorgeous city, shall not my petty affair be as nothing, when I behold in Hautboy the vine and the rose climbing the shattered shafts of his tumbled temple of Fame?"

Next day I tore all my manuscripts, bought me a fiddle, and went to take regular lessons of Hautboy.

5 狄更斯《兒童的故事》
──資本文明社會的人道寫實先驅

小說特徵

工業社會底層人物的困境、都市問題、監獄、貧富差距

查爾斯・狄更斯
(Charles Dickens, 1812-1870)

This is the best of the time, this is the worst of the time.
-Charles Dickens, A Tale of Two Cities

這是最好的時刻,也是最壞的時刻。

──查爾斯・狄更斯《雙城記》

作者短評

狄更斯（Charles Dickens），1812年，出生於英國樸次茅斯，父親約翰·狄更斯因無力償還舉債，被捕下獄，一家人隨著父親遷至牢房居住，狄更斯也因此被送到倫敦一家鞋油店，每天工作10個小時。或許是由於這段經歷，備嘗艱辛、屈辱，看盡人情冷暖，使得狄更斯的作品更關注底層社會的生活狀態。

狄更斯並沒有接受很多的正規教育，是靠自學成才。狄更斯後來成為《晨報》的國會記者，專門採訪英國下議院的政策辯論，也時常環遊英倫採訪各種選舉活動，甚至前往他所嚮往的美國，他在美國的見聞被收進其在1842年出版的《美國紀行》，並在美國享有極大的聲望及影響力，可以說美國十九世紀以後，批判資本功利歪風的寫實小說，無不受狄更斯的啟發與繼承。

1849年他出版了自傳題材的小說《塊肉餘生錄》，這部小說的內容與狄更斯的個人經歷有很大關係，是狄更斯的代表作。狄更斯以後的小說顯得更為尖銳並具批判性，著名的有《雙城記》。

狄更斯一生刻苦勤勉，繁重的勞動和對改革現實的失望，嚴重損害了他的健康。1870年6月9日狄更斯因腦溢血與世長辭，被安葬在西敏寺，他的墓碑上如此寫道：「他是貧窮、受苦與被壓迫人民的同情者；他的去世令世界失去了一位偉大的英國作家。」

作品分析

英國至維多利亞時期（1819-1891），工業革命的領先，國力雖達鼎盛，卻也因人民貧富差距拉大而生「兩個國度的問題」（The issue of nations），社會改革運動乘勢而起。影響於文學者，也宣告英國浪漫主義時代的結束，而狄更斯的寫實主義作品，正是英國維多利亞時期最有代表性作家，他小說中對弱勢小民的苦楚與貧窮的揭露，往往間接促成社會的改革。也因此，狄更斯的小說充滿倫敦都市生活的描述，寫出他對市井生活的深刻觀察，首開先例讓人注意到都市民生問題，狄更斯小說對當時資本主義快速發展的英國社會批判冷漠疏離功利至上的氛圍，他將社會正義的意識置入文學，大加制衡十九世紀資本文明越來越窄化人性的問題，是狄更斯對小說的最大貢獻。

今年正逢狄更斯兩百週年誕生紀念，狄更斯《兒童的故事》敘述了一位旅人，在途中，見證一位兒童自少年、青年、紳士到老年的一步步成長，旅人並在每一階段，陪他玩樂、學習、工作，再看他成家、生子、立業，最後歸於塵土。簡單的描述人的一生段落不過如此，生命就是如此的單調與滿足，宛如一幅人生畫卷，兼具幽默、批判與溫暖。狄更斯也碰觸了死亡的探討，他將人生的每一個階段的結束－如兒童到少年，不一定是死亡，其實是另段的開始，不需如旅人那般的失落及驚訝，即便到了盡頭，生命的過程也是延續的，我們不過是生命循環中的一位接棒人罷了！

The Child's Story

by Charles Dickens

Once upon a time, a good many years ago, there was a traveler, and he set out upon a journey. It was a magic journey, and was to seem very long when he began it, and very short when he got half way through.

He travelled along a rather dark path for some little time, without meeting anything, until at last he came to a beautiful child. So he said to the child, "What do you do here?" And the child said, "I am always at play. Come and play with me!"

So, he played with that child, the whole day long, and they were very merry. The sky was so blue, the sun was so bright, the water was so sparkling, the leaves were so green, the flowers were so lovely, and they heard such singing-birds and saw so many butteries, that everything was beautiful. This was in fine weather. When it rained, they loved to watch the falling drops, and to smell the fresh scents. When it blew, it was delightful to listen to the wind, and fancy what it said, as it came rushing from its home--where was that, they wondered! -whistling and howling, driving the clouds before it, bending the trees, rumbling in the chimneys, shaking the house, and making the sea roar in fury. But, when it snowed, that was best of all; for, they liked nothing so well as to look up at the white flakes falling fast and thick, like down from the breasts of millions of white birds; and to see how smooth and deep the drift was; and to listen to the hush upon the paths and roads.

They had plenty of the finest toys in the world, and the most astonishing picture-books: all about scimitars and slippers and turbans, and dwarfs and giants and genii and fairies, and blue- beards and bean-stalks and riches and caverns and forests and Valentines and Orsons: and all new and all true.

But, one day, of a sudden, the traveler lost the child. He called to him over and over again, but got no answer. So, he went upon his road, and went on for a little while without meeting anything, until at last he came to a handsome boy. So, he said to the boy, "What do you do here?" And the boy said, "I am always learning. Come and learn with me."

So he learned with that boy about Jupiter and Juno, and the Greeks and the Romans, and I don't know what, and learned more than I could tell--or he either, for he soon forgot a great deal of it. But, they were not always learning; they had the merriest games that ever were played. They rowed upon the river in summer, and skated on the ice in winter; they were active afoot, and active on horseback; at cricket, and all games at ball; at prisoner's base, hare and hounds, follow my leader, and more sports than I can think of; nobody could beat them. They had holidays too, and Twelfth cakes, and parties where they danced till midnight, and real Theatres where they saw palaces of real gold and silver rise out of the real earth, and saw all the wonders of the world at once. As to friends, they had such dear friends and so many of them, that I want the time to reckon them up. They were all young, like the handsome boy, and were never to be strange to one another all their lives through.

Still, one day, in the midst of all these pleasures, the traveler lost the boy as he had lost the child, and, after calling to him in vain, went on upon his journey. So he went on for a little while without seeing anything, until at last he came to a young man. So, he said to the young man, "What do you do here?" And the young man said, "I am always in love. Come and love with me."

So, he went away with that young man, and presently they came to one of the prettiest girls that ever was seen--just like Fanny in the corner there--and she had eyes like Fanny, and hair like Fanny, and dimples like Fanny's, and she laughed and coloured just as Fanny does while I am talking about her. So, the young man fell in love directly--just as Somebody I won't mention, the first time he came here, did with Fanny. Well! he was teased sometimes--just as Somebody used to be by Fanny; and they quarreled sometimes--just as Somebody and Fanny used to quarrel; and they made it up, and sat in the dark, and wrote letters every day, and never were happy asunder, and were always looking out for one another and pretending not to, and were engaged at Christmas-time, and sat close to one another by the fire, and were going to be married very soon--all exactly like Somebody I won't mention, and Fanny!

But, the traveler lost them one day, as he had lost the rest of his friends, and, after calling to them to come back, which they never did, went on upon his journey. So, he went on for a little while without seeing anything, until at last he came to a middle-aged gentleman. So, he said to the gentleman, "What are you doing here?" And his answer was, "I am always busy. Come and be busy with me!"

So, he began to be very busy with that gentleman, and they went on through the wood together. The whole journey was through a wood, only it had been open and green at first, like a wood in spring; and now began to be thick and dark, like a wood in summer; some of the little trees that had come out earliest, were even turning brown. The gentleman was not alone, but had a lady of about the same age with him, who was his Wife; and they had children, who were with them too. So, they all went on together through the wood, cutting down the trees, and making a path through the branches and the fallen leaves, and carrying burdens, and working hard.

Sometimes, they came to a long green avenue that opened into deeper woods. Then they would hear a very little, distant voice crying, "Father, father, I am another child! Stop for me!" And presently they would see a very little figure, growing larger as it came along, running to join them. When it came up, they all crowded round it, and kissed and welcomed it; and then they all went on together.

Sometimes, they came to several avenues at once, and then they all stood still, and one of the children said, "Father, I am going to sea," and another said, "Father, I am going to India," and another, "Father, I am going to seek my fortune where I can," and another, "Father, I am going to Heaven!" So, with many tears at parting, they went, solitary, down those avenues, each child upon its way; and the child who went to Heaven, rose into the golden air and vanished.

Whenever these partings happened, the traveler looked at the gentleman, and saw him glance up at the sky above the trees, where the day was beginning to decline, and the sunset to come on. He saw, too, that his hair was turning grey. But, they never could rest long, for they had their journey to perform, and it was necessary for them to be always busy.

At last, there had been so many partings that there were no children left, and only the traveller, the gentleman, and the lady, went upon their way in company. And now the wood was yellow; and now brown; and the leaves, even of the forest trees, began to fall. So, they came to an avenue that was darker than the rest, and were pressing forward on their journey without looking down it when the lady stopped.

"My husband," said the lady. "I am called."

They listened, and they heard a voice a long way down the avenue, say, "Mother, mother!"

It was the voice of the first child who had said, "I am going to Heaven!" and the father said, "I pray not yet. The sunset is very near. I pray not yet!"

But, the voice cried, "Mother, mother!" without minding him, though his hair was now quite white, and tears were on his face.

Then, the mother, who was already drawn into the shade of the dark avenue and moving away with her arms still round his neck, kissed him, and said, "My dearest, I am summoned, and I go!" And she was gone. And the traveler and he were left alone together.

And they went on and on together, until they came to very near the end of the wood: so near, that they could see the sunset shining red before them through the trees.

Yet, once more, while he broke his way among the branches, the traveler lost his friend. He called and called, but there was no reply, and when he passed out of the wood, and saw the peaceful sun going down upon a wide purple prospect, he came to an old man sitting on a fallen tree. So, he said to the old man, "What do you do here?" And the old man said with a calm smile, "I am always remembering. Come and remember with me!"

So the traveler sat down by the side of that old man, face to face with the serene sunset; and all his friends came softly back and stood around him. The beautiful child, the handsome boy, the young man in love, the father, mother, and children: every one of them was there, and he had lost nothing. So, he loved them all, and was kind and forbearing with them all, and was always pleased to watch them all, and they all honoured and loved him. And I think the traveler must be yourself, dear Grandfather, because this what you do to us, and what we do to you.

6 安布魯・畢爾斯《梟河橋記事》 ——戰爭下的人性扭曲

小說特徵

戰爭與超自然手法的人性展現

安布魯・畢爾斯
（Ambrose G. Bierce, 1842-1913）

War was the making of Bierce as a man and a writer. [From his grim experience, he became] truly capable of transferring the bloody, headless bodies and boar-eaten corpses of the battlefield onto paper.

-Biographer Richard O'Conner

戰爭造就了畢爾斯為個人與作家。來自戰爭的殘酷經驗，他得以將戰場屍首的血肉模糊，傳達於文章之上。

——傳記作家　李察・歐康諾

作者短評

　　安布魯・畢爾斯（Ambrose Bierce），1842年，出生於俄亥俄州，成長在印地安那州，兩地在美國當時雖是西進運動的拓荒之地，但畢爾斯遺傳父母文學喜好，也愛上寫作。1861年美國南北內戰爆發，畢爾斯隨即加入了北方部隊，在他服役的四年間，衝鋒陷陣，戰場廝殺，他頭部曾嚴重受傷，最後以少校軍銜退役。戰後，畢爾斯專職於舊金山報社擔任報紙專欄作家，由於文風嘲諷，讓他贏得「辛辣畢爾斯（Bitter Bierce）」之封號。

　　畢爾斯的小說多以親身參與之美國內戰為題材，並由戰爭探索人性的旨味，他許多傑出的短篇故事都是以南北戰爭的恐怖經驗為主題，細節寫實逼真，加上畢爾斯是講述超自然故事的能手，這將戰場結合靈異想像的架構，結局常現毛骨悚然及驚駭效果，《梟河橋記事》（*An Occurrence at Owl Creek Bridge*）公認是畢爾斯創造恐怖氣氛及結局高潮之絕佳範例。

　　畢爾斯晚年深受戰時受傷後遺症與氣喘之苦。1913年，畢爾斯前往墨西哥，想要獨家採訪當地革命叛亂，從此，音信杳然，據信是被叛軍所害，成為美國最出名的文學家失蹤案例之一。

作品分析

　　在許榮哲的〈小說課〉提到，一般小說的敘事流程，都是基於事實的前提，引領讀者進入一步步安排的情節，最後在真相答案的揭曉下，畫下結局。但是，想像一下，如果你發現引領你進入故事的敘事者，從頭到尾都在說謊，結果你不但不氣憤，反而感動？可會是什麼的小說創意情況。在畢爾斯的《梟河橋記事》就提供了此一類屬的小說典範，百分之九十九的內容，集中敘述：南軍士兵Peyton Farquhar被北軍俘虜，綁在鐵橋上要吊死時，意外發生了，繩索斷裂，Peyton Farquhar掉到河裡，展開他一連串的「回家」逃亡，閃過追捕他的槍林彈雨，再掙脫漩渦激流，艱苦上岸，馬不停啼地跑了一天一夜，他又累又餓，但一想到妻子，馬上又加緊腳步，最後終於回到了家，高貴的妻子在晨光明朗的家門口迎接，就要抱住她時……。目前為止，畢爾斯精準捕捉了戰爭氣氛，刻劃出Farquhar個人在戰爭中的強烈不安與死亡的恐懼，交纏著求生與親情的饑渴，當所有人正感動於主角即將與妻子團聚時，令人驚心恐怖的高峰，卻在終了瞬間畫下：

> 他突然感到項頸被猛然一擊，盡起灼熱目眩的白光，然後一切歸於暗黑、寂靜。Peyton Farquhar死了，斷了項頸的屍體在梟溪橋下來回地盪來盪去。

畢爾斯等於寫出了主角心靈的渴望，不顧時空、生理的物理限制，看到了不存在的「身體逃亡」，而不是選擇以「靈魂逃亡」的鬼片方式處理，正因為主角強烈要回家見他妻子最後一面，所以他回家不但合理，只要人同此心，儘管真相是一切都沒有發生，小說不但可以不必向科學負責，還讓讀者感動、

叫好。畢爾斯此一扭曲時空、真實謊言的創意，從此蔚為風
行，成了小說、電影創作的法寶，前些時，由布魯斯威利斯所
主演電影〈神鬼第六感〉、妮可基曼〈靈異第六感〉、〈蘇西
的世界〉都是基於此一構想的作品。

文選閱讀

An Occurrence at Owl Creek Bridge

by Ambrose Bierce

I

A man stood upon a railroad bridge in northern Alabama, looking
down into the swift water twenty feet below. The man's hands were behind
his back, the wrists bound with a cord. A rope closely encircled his neck. It
was attached to a stout timber above his head and the slack fell to the level
of his knees…his executioners--two private soldiers of the Federal army,
directed by a sergeant who in civil life may have been a deputy sheriff. At
a short remove upon the same temporary platform was an officer in the
uniform of his rank, armed. He was a captain…The captain stood with
folded arms, silent, observing the work of his subordinates, but making no
sign. Death is a dignitary who when he comes announced is to be received
with formal manifestations of respect, even by those most familiar with him.
In the code of military etiquette silence and fixity are forms of deference.

The man who was engaged in being hanged was apparently about thirty-five years of age. He was a civilian, if one might judge from his habit, which was that of a planter. His features were good--a straight nose, firm mouth, broad forehead, from which his long, dark hair was combed straight back, falling behind his ears to the collar of his well-fitting frock coat. He wore a mustache and pointed beard, but no whiskers; his eyes were large and dark gray, and had a kindly expression which one would hardly have expected in one whose neck was in the hemp. Evidently this was no vulgar assassin. The liberal military code makes provision for hanging many kinds of persons, and gentlemen are not excluded.

The preparations being complete, the two private soldiers stepped aside and each drew away the plank upon which he had been standing. The sergeant turned to the captain, saluted and placed himself immediately behind that officer, who in turn moved apart one pace. These movements left the condemned man and the sergeant standing on the two ends of the same plank, which spanned three of the cross-ties of the bridge. The end upon which the civilian stood almost, but not quite, reached a fourth. This plank had been held in place by the weight of the captain; it was now held by that of the sergeant. At a signal from the former the latter would step aside, the plank would tilt and the condemned man go down between two ties. The arrangement commended itself to his judgment as simple and effective. His face had not been covered nor his eyes bandaged. He looked a moment at his "unsteadfast footing," then let his gaze wander to the swirling water of the stream racing madly beneath his feet. A piece of dancing driftwood caught his attention and his eyes followed it down the current. How slowly it appeared to move, What a sluggish stream!

He closed his eyes in order to fix his last thoughts upon his wife and children. The water, touched to gold by the early sun, the brooding mists under the banks at some distance down the stream, the fort, the soldiers, the piece of drift--all had distracted him. And now he became conscious of a new disturbance. Striking through the thought of his dear ones was a sound which he could neither ignore nor understand, a sharp, distinct, metallic percussion like the stroke of a blacksmith's hammer upon the anvil; it had the same ringing quality. He wondered what it was, and whether immeasurably distant or near by--it seemed both. Its recurrence was regular, but as slow as the tolling of a death knell. He awaited each stroke with impatience and--he knew not why--apprehension. The intervals of silence grew progressively longer, the delays became maddening. With their greater infrequency the sounds increased in strength and sharpness. They hurt his ear like the thrust of a knife; he feared he would shriek. What he heard was the ticking of his watch.

He unclosed his eyes and saw again the water below him. "If I could free my hands," he thought, "I might throw off the noose and spring into the stream. By diving I could evade the bullets and, swimming vigorously, reach the bank, take to the woods and get away home. My home, thank God, is as yet outside their lines; my wife and little ones are still beyond the invader's farthest advance."

As these thoughts, which have here to be set down in words, were flashed into the doomed man's brain rather than evolved from it the captain nodded to the sergeant. The sergeant stepped aside.

II

Peyton Farquhar was a well-to-do planter, of an old and highly respected Alabama family. Being a slave owner and like other slave owners a politician he was naturally an original secessionist and ardently devoted to the Southern cause. Circumstances of an imperious nature, which it is unnecessary to relate here, had prevented him from taking service with the gallant army that had fought the disastrous campaigns ending with the fall of Corinth, and he chafed under the inglorious restraint, longing for the release of his energies, the larger life of the soldier, the opportunity for distinction. That opportunity, he felt, would come, as it comes to all in war time. Meanwhile he did what he could. No service was too humble for him to perform in aid of the South, no adventure too perilous for him to undertake if consistent with the character of a civilian who was at heart a soldier, and who in good faith that all is fair in love and war.

One evening while Farquhar and his wife were sitting on a rustic bench near the entrance to his grounds, a gray-clad soldier rode up to the gate and asked for a drink of water. Mrs. Farquhar was only toe, happy to serve him with her own white hands. While she was fetching the water her husband approached the dusty horseman and inquired eagerly for news from the front.

"The Yanks are repairing the railroads," said the man, "and are getting ready for another advance. They have reached the Owl Creek bridge, put it in order and built a stockade on the north bank. The commandant has issued an order, which is posted everywhere, declaring that any civilian caught interfering with the railroad, its bridges, tunnels or trains will be summarily hanged. I saw the order."

"How far is it to the Owl Creek bridge?" Farquhar asked.

"About thirty miles."

"Is there no force on this side the creek?"

"Only a picket post half a mile out, on the railroad, and a single sentinel at this end of the bridge."

"Suppose a man--a civilian and student of hanging--should elude the picket post and perhaps get the better of the sentinel," said Farquhar, smiling, "what could he accomplish?"

The soldier reflected. "I was there a month ago," he replied. "I observed that the flood of last winter had lodged a great quantity of driftwood against the wooden pier at this end of the bridge. It is now dry and would burn like tow."

The lady had now brought the water, which the soldier drank. He thanked her ceremoniously, bowed to her husband and rode away. An hour later, after nightfall, he repassed the plantation, going northward in the direction from which he had come. He was a Federal scout.

III

As Peyton Farquhar fell straight downward through the bridge he lost consciousness and was as one already dead. From this state he was awakened--ages later, it seemed to him--by the pain of a sharp pressure upon his throat, followed by a sense of suffocation. They seemed like streams of fire heating him to an intolerable temperature. As to his head, he was conscious of nothing but a feeling of fulness--of congestion. These sensations were unaccompanied by thought. He was conscious of motion. Encompassed in a luminous cloud, he swung like a vast pendulum. Then all at once, ...The power of thought was restored; he knew that the rope had broken and he had fallen into the stream. There was no additional strangulation; the noose about his neck was already suffocating him and kept the water from his lungs. To die of hanging at the bottom of a river!--the idea seemed to him ludicrous. He opened his eyes in the darkness and saw above him a gleam of light, but how distant, how inaccessible! He was still sinking, for the light became fainter and fainter until it was a mere glimmer. Then it began to grow and brighten, and he knew that he was rising toward the surface--knew it with reluctance, for he was now very comfortable. "To be hanged and drowned," he thought? "that is not so bad; but I do not wish to be shot. No; I will not be shot; that is not fair."

He was not conscious of an effort, but a sharp pain in his wrist apprised him that he was trying to free his hands. The cord fell away; his arms parted and floated upward, the hands dimly seen on each side in the growing light. He watched them with a new interest as first one and then the other pounced upon the noose at his neck. They tore it away and thrust it fiercely aside, its undulations resembling those of a water snake. "Put it back, put it back!" He thought he shouted these words to his hands, for the undoing of the noose had been succeeded by the direst pang that he had yet experienced. His neck ached horribly; his brain was on fire; his heart, which had been fluttering faintly, gave a great leap, trying to force itself out at his mouth. His whole body was racked and wrenched with an insupportable anguish! But his disobedient hands gave no heed to the command. They beat the water vigorously with quick, downward strokes, forcing him to the surface. He felt his head emerge; his eyes were blinded by the sunlight; his chest expanded convulsively, and with a supreme and crowning agony his lungs engulfed a great draught of air, which instantly he expelled in a shriek!

He was now in full possession of his physical senses. They were, indeed, preternaturally keen and alert. Something in the awful disturbance of his organic system had so exalted and refined them that they made record of things never before perceived. He felt the ripples upon his face and heard their separate sounds as they struck. He looked at the forest on the bank of the stream, saw the individual trees, the leaves and the veining of each leaf--saw the very insects upon them: the locusts, the brilliant-bodied flies, the grey spiders stretching their webs from twig to twig. He noted the prismatic colors in all the dewdrops upon a million blades of grass. The humming of the gnats that danced above the eddies of the stream, the beating of the dragon flies' wings, the strokes of the water-spiders' legs, like oars which had lifted their boat--all these made audible music. A fish slid along beneath his eyes and he heard the rush of its body parting the water.

He had come to the surface facing down the stream; in a moment the visible world seemed to wheel slowly round, himself the pivotal point, and he saw the bridge, the fort, the soldiers upon the bridge, the captain, the sergeant, the two privates, his executioners. They were in silhouette against the blue sky. They shouted and gesticulated, pointing at him. The captain had drawn his pistol, but did not fire; the others were unarmed. Their movements were grotesque and horrible, their forms gigantic.

Suddenly he heard a sharp report and something struck the water smartly within a few inches of his head, spattering his face with spray. He heard a second report, and saw one of the sentinels with his rifle at his shoulder, a light cloud of blue smoke rising from the muzzle. The man in the water saw the eye of the man on the bridge gazing into his own through the sights of the rifle. He observed that it was a grey eye and remembered having read that grey eyes were keenest, and that all famous marksmen had them. Nevertheless, this one had missed.

A counter-swirl had caught Farquhar and turned him half round; he was again looking into the forest on the bank opposite the fort. The sound of a clear, high voice in a monotonous singsong now rang out behind him and came across the water with a distinctness that pierced and subdued all other sounds, even the beating of the ripples in his ears. Although no soldier, he had frequented camps enough to know the dread significance of that deliberate, drawling, aspirated chant; the lieu. tenant on shore was taking a part in the morning's work. How coldly and pitilessly--with what an even, calm intonation, presaging, and enforcing tranquility in the men-- with what accurately measured inter vals fell those cruel words:

"Attention, company!...Shoulder arms!...Ready!...Aim!...Fire!"

Farquhar dived--dived as deeply as he could. The water roared in his ears like the voice of Niagara, yet he heard the dulled thunder of the volley and, rising again toward the surface, met shining bits of metal, singularly flattened, oscillating slowly downward. Some of them touched him on the face and hands, then fell away, continuing their descent. One lodged between his collar and neck; it was uncomfortably warm and he snatched it out.

As he rose to the surface, gasping for breath, he saw that he had been a long time under water; he was perceptibly farther down stream nearer to safety. The soldiers had almost finished reloading; the metal ramrods flashed all at once in the sunshine as they were drawn from the barrels, turned in the air, and thrust into their sockets. The two sentinels fired again, independently and ineffectually.

The hunted man saw all this over his shoulder; he was now swimming vigorously with the current. His brain was as energetic as his arms and legs; he thought with the rapidity of lightning.

"The officer," he reasoned, "will not make that martinet's error a second time. It is as easy to dodge a volley as a single shot. He has probably already given the command to fire at will. God help me, I cannot dodge them all!"

A rising sheet of water curved over him, fell down upon him, blinded him, strangled him! The cannon had taken a hand in the game. As he shook his head free from the commotion of the smitten water he heard the deflected shot humming through the air ahead, and in an instant it was cracking and smashing the branches in the forest beyond.

Suddenly he felt himself whirled round and round--spinning like a top. The water, the banks, the forests, the now distant bridge, fort and men--all were commingled and blurred. Objects were represented by their colors only; circular horizontal streaks of color--that was all he saw.

He had been caught in a vortex and was being whirled on with a velocity of advance and gyration that made him giddy and sick. In a few moments he was flung upon the gravel at the foot of the left bank of the stream--the southern bank--and behind a projecting point which concealed him from his enemies.

A whiz and rattle of grapeshot among the branches high above his head roused him from his dream. The baffled cannoneer had fired him a random farewell. He sprang to his feet, rushed up the sloping bank, and plunged into the forest.

All that day he traveled, laying his course by the rounding sun. The forest seemed interminable; nowhere did he discover a break in it, not even a woodman's road. He had not known that he lived in so wild a region. There was something uncanny in the revelation.

By nightfall he was fatigued, footsore, famishing. The thought of his wife and children urged him on. At last he found a road which led him in what he knew to be the right direction. It was as wide and straight as a city street, yet it seemed untraveled. No fields bordered it, no dwelling anywhere. Not so much as the barking of a dog suggested human habitation. The black bodies of the trees formed a straight wall on both sides, terminating on the horizon in a point, like a diagram in a lesson in perspective. Overhead, as he looked up through this rift in the wood, shone great garden stars looking unfamiliar and grouped in strange constellations. He was sure they were arranged in some order which had a secret and malign significance. The wood on either side was full of singular noises, among which--once, twice, and again--he distinctly heard whispers in an unknown tongue.

Doubtless, despite his suffering, he had fallen asleep while walking, for now he sees another scene--perhaps he has merely recovered from a delirium. He stands at the gate of his own home. All is as he left it, and all bright and beautiful in the morning sunshine. He must have traveled the entire night. As he pushes open the gate and passes up the wide white walk, he sees a flutter of female garments; his wife, looking fresh and cool and sweet, steps down from the veranda to meet him. At the bottom of the steps she stands waiting, with a smile of ineffable joy, an attitude of matchless grace and dignity. Ah, how beautiful she is! He springs forward with extended arms. As he is about to clasp her he feels a stunning blow upon the back of the neck; a blinding white light blazes all about him with a sound like the shock of a cannon--then all is darkness and silence!

Peyton Farquhar was dead; his body, with a broken neck, swung gently from side to side beneath the timbers of the Owl Creek bridge.

7 傑克‧倫敦《生火》
——自然中的人性原始力

小說特徵

社會達爾文思想與自然主義的人性衝突

傑克‧倫敦
(Jack London, 1876-1916)

It did not lead him to meditate upon his frailty as a creature of temperature, and upon man's frailty in general, able only to live within certain narrow limits of heat and cold; and from there on it did not lead him to the conjectural field of immortality and man's place in the universe.

-Jack London, To Build A Fire

他只是覺得寒冷難過而已,並沒有引起他去思索自己以及一般人類的脆弱,人是有體溫的生靈,只能生存在有限的寒暑之內,更別說他還能思考至永恆的範疇以及人類在宇宙中的地位。

——傑克‧倫敦,《生火》

作者短評

　　傑克・倫敦（Jack London），1876年，出生於美國加州舊金山。自童年起，傑克・倫敦便飽嘗了貧困的滋味，靠自學，當童工維生。1890年，倫敦滿十四歲，雖然脫離童工限制，進入罐頭廠工作，但一天十小時工作，而每小時的工資不超過十美分；之後，傑克・倫敦失業，輾轉流浪於美國和加拿大各大都市的貧民窟。

　　1890年代是美國資本主義與達爾文理論的無縫接軌結合，表面是「公平競爭，自由放任」的高尚動人，實則是冷血現實地奉「弱肉強食，適者生存」為金科玉律。這也促成自幼苦嘗美國資本家剝削殘酷的傑克・倫敦成為鬥志昂揚的社會主義信徒，熱心美國工人運動，倫敦在公共圖書館學習達爾文、馬克思、尼采的著作，他用一年的時間學完了中學四年的課程，順利考入位於伯克利的加州大學，這時他已經二十歲了，但四個月後，就被學校退學，倫敦前往阿拉斯加淘金，旅程中的經歷和觀察，幫助他寫下了美國文學史上的經典之作《野性的呼喚》（*The Call of the Wild*）與稍後的《狼牙》（*White Fang*）。

　　傑克・倫敦從小就對動物懷有深厚的感情，所創作一系列的冒險小說，狼犬自然成了他作品不可或缺的主角與象徵，如《狼牙》與《野性的呼喚》：敘述一隻狼狗逐漸習慣人類世界，最後甚至犧牲性命以挽救主人生命的感人故事。《生火》可視為《野性的呼喚》姐妹篇。這一系列由冰天雪地、旅人與狼犬所組合的求生探險卡司，兼顧自然與寫實主義的手法，旅途中，人與自然以及人與狗之間情節，構成傑克‧倫敦小說的「北國法典」（London's Code of Northland），人類如野獸般掙扎求生的內容，看似與達爾文的「弱肉強食，適者生存」呼應，實則隱喻資本主義社會的殘酷無情和對金錢的崇拜，讓人性之同情心和無私變成了血腥慾望，沒有互助與奉獻，這種殘酷法典之最終結局便是自我毀滅。

傑克‧倫敦在1916年1月，他脫離了美國社會黨；11月22日，離世，據信是服用過量麻醉藥品自殺。

作品分析

傑克‧倫敦創作目的與動機，深受1890年代美國資本主義社會背景下，一生苦澀經驗大有關係。美國資本主義思想產生，基礎是混合了美國清教「工作倫理」（work ethics）之傳統信仰、工商革命的擴張現實，加以達爾文「適者生存」理論與美式民主的全面結合、互用；財富成為衡量一個人的標準，資本家如「鋼鐵大王」卡內基或「石油大王」洛克斐勒代表了人生成功的典範，這時顛沛流離的傑克‧倫敦則成了社會定義下的失敗者。

傑克‧倫敦代表作《生火》是以一個危險旅程而鋪展，描寫一個迷途的旅人，誤判形勢之下，遭受暴風雪侵襲，在樹下用最後的一根火柴生火求生，火終於生了起來，就在旅人正要鬆口氣之際，火苗的熱氣上升，溶化了樹枝上的一堆積雪，雪掉落下來，把火堆澆息，在此打擊之下，旅人已喪失求生意志，便乾脆坐著等死。其實，小說重點不在於主角的最後凍死，而在於他對事物的本質認識不當，結果付出生命的代價。

　　倫敦筆下，酷寒不過是一個象徵人類所不能察覺經驗範疇的暗喻，而人在大自然裡，注重官能、講究理性，以現實為引導，眼光的短淺，而萎縮了古老、難以言諭的本能引導。這在《生火》主角過於自信經驗研判路線，當踏入伏冰下的積水，生火求生一再的失誤，這時主角對自己理性構思下，自然世界是井然有序的信心也就消失了，說穿了，他自以為是的智能是無用武之地，相反地，狗的本能就佔了優勢。這也是傑克・倫敦好用自然主義的敘事手法，表面描寫人與動物、人與環境的抗爭，實則表達人與動物在大自然生存抗爭的那種原始慾望與動能，由於每個故事都有他親身經歷，方能有如此身歷其境的貼切，表現出他自然主義寫作的粗獷風格與自然無情的悲劇性。倫敦認為，在一個冷漠而無情的環境中，人性的原始力遠比智能，更有價值。

To Build A Fire

by Jack London

DAY HAD BROKEN cold and gray, exceedingly cold and gray, ... It was nine o'clock. There was no sun nor hint of sun, though there was not a cloud in the sky. This fact did not worry the man. He was used to the lack of sun. It had been days since he had seen the sun.

The man flung a look back along the way he had come. The Yukon lay a mile wide and hidden under three feet of ice. On top of this ice were as many feet of snow. It was all pure white. North and south, as far as his eye could see, it was unbroken white, save for a dark hair-line. This dark hair-line was the trail--the main trail--that led north seventy miles to Dawson, and still on to the north a thousand miles to Nulato, and finally to St. Michael on Bering Sea, a thousand miles and half a thousand more.

But all this--the mysterious, far-reaching hair-line trail, the absence of sun from the sky, the tremendous cold, and the strangeness and weirdness of it all--made no impression on the man. It was not because he was long used to it. He was a newcomer in the land, a *chechaquo*, and this was his first winter. The trouble with him was that he was without imagination. He was quick and alert in the things of life, but only in the things, and not in the significances. Fifty degrees below zero meant eighty-odd degrees of frost. Such fact impressed him as being cold and uncomfortable, and that was all. It did not lead him to meditate upon his frailty as a creature of temperature, and upon man's frailty in general, able only to live within certain narrow limits of heat and cold; and from there on it did not lead him to the conjectural field of immortality and man's place in the universe. Fifty degrees below zero stood for a bite of frost that hurt and that must be guarded against by the use of mittens, ear-flaps, warm moccasins, and thick socks. Fifty degrees below zero was to him just precisely fifty degrees below zero. That there should be anything more to it than that was a thought that never entered his head.

As he turned to go on, he spat speculatively. There was a sharp, explosive crackle that startled him. He spat again. And again, in the air, before it could fall to the snow, the spittle crackled. He knew that at fifty below spittle crackled on the snow, but this spittle had crackled in the air. Undoubtedly it was colder than fifty below--how much colder he did not know...He plunged in among the big spruce trees. The trail was faint. A foot of snow had fallen since the last sled had passed over, and he was glad he was without a sled, traveling light. In fact, he carried nothing but the lunch wrapped in the handkerchief. He was surprised, however, at the cold. It certainly was cold, he concluded, as he rubbed his numb nose and cheek-bones with his mittened hand. He was a warm-whiskered man, but the hair on his face did not protect the high cheek-bones and the eager nose that thrust itself aggressively into the frosty air.

At the man's heels trotted a dog, a big native husky, the proper wolf-dog, gray-coated and without any visible or temperamental difference from its brother, the wild wolf. The animal was depressed by the tremendous cold. It knew that it was no time for traveling. Its instinct told it a truer tale than was told to the man by the man's judgment. In reality, it was not merely colder than fifty below zero; it was colder than sixty below, than seventy below. It was seventy-five below zero. The dog did not know anything about thermometers. Possibly in its brain there was no sharp consciousness of a condition of very cold such as was in the man's brain. But the brute had its instinct. The dog had learned fire, and it wanted fire, or else to burrow under the snow and cuddle its warmth away from the air.

Empty as the man's mind was of thoughts, he was keenly observant, and he noticed the changes in the creek, the curves and bends and timber-jams, and always he sharply noted where he placed his feet. The creek he knew was frozen clear to the bottom,--no creek could contain water in that arctic winter,--but he knew also that there were springs that bubbled out from the hillsides and ran along under the snow and on top the ice of the creek. They were traps. They hid pools of water under the snow that might be three inches deep, or three feet. Sometimes a skin of ice half an inch thick covered them, and in turn was covered by the snow. Sometimes there were alternate layers of water and ice-skin, so that when one broke through he kept on breaking through for a while, sometimes wetting himself to the waist.

In the course of the next two hours he came upon several similar traps. Usually the snow above the hidden pools had a sunken, candied appearance that advertised the danger. Once again, however, he had a close call; and once, suspecting danger,...and for half an hour the man saw no signs of any. And then it happened. At a place where there were no signs, where the soft, unbroken snow seemed to advertise solidity beneath, the man broke through. It was not deep. He wet himself halfway to the knees before he floundered out to the firm crust.

He was angry, and cursed his luck aloud. He had hoped to get into camp with the boys at six o'clock, and this would delay him an hour, for he would have to build a fire and dry out his foot-gear. This was imperative at that low temperature--he knew that much; and he turned aside to the bank, which he climbed. The flame he got by touching a match to a small shred of birch-bark that he took from his pocket. This burned even more readily than paper. Placing it on the foundation, he fed the young flame with wisps of dry grass and with the tiniest dry twigs.

He worked slowly and carefully, keenly aware of his danger. Gradually, as the flame grew stronger, he increased the size of the twigs with which he fed it. He squatted in the snow, pulling the twigs out from their entanglement in the brush and feeding directly to the flame. He knew there must be no failure. When it is seventy-five below zero, a man must not fail in his first attempt to build a fire--that is, if his feet are wet. If his feet are dry, and he fails, he can run along the trail for half a mile and restore his circulation. But the circulation of wet and freezing feet cannot be restored by running when it is seventy-five below. No matter how fast he runs, the wet feet will freeze the harder.

But he was safe. Toes and nose and cheeks would be only touched by the frost, for the fire was beginning to burn with strength. He was feeding it with twigs the size of his finger. In another minute he would be able to feed it with branches the size of his wrist, and then he could remove his wet foot-gear, and, while it dried, he could keep his naked feet warm by the fire, rubbing them at first, of course, with snow. The fire was a success. He was safe.

There was the fire, snapping and crackling and promising life with every dancing flame. He started to untie his moccasins. They were coated with ice; the thick German socks were like sheaths of iron halfway to the knees; and the moccasin strings were like rods of steel all twisted and knotted as by some conflagration. For a moment he tugged with his numb fingers, then, realizing the folly of it, he drew his sheath-knife.

But before he could cut the strings, it happened. It was his own fault or, rather, his mistake. He should not have built the fire under the spruce tree. He should have built it in the open. But it had been easier to pull the twigs from the brush and drop them directly on the fire. Now the tree under which he had done this carried a weight of snow on its boughs. No wind had blown for weeks, and each bough was fully freighted. Each time he had pulled a twig he had communicated a slight agitation to the tree- -an imperceptible agitation, so far as he was concerned, but an agitation sufficient to bring about the disaster. High up in the tree one bough capsized its load of snow. This fell on the boughs beneath, capsizing them. This process continued, spreading out and involving the whole tree. It grew like an avalanche, and it descended without warning upon the man and the fire, and the fire was blotted out! Where it had burned was a mantle of fresh and disordered snow.

The man was shocked. It was as though he had just heard his own sentence of death. For a moment he sat and stared at the spot where the fire had been. Then he grew very calm. If he had only had a trail-mate he would have been in no danger now. The trail-mate could have built the fire. Well, it was up to him to build the fire over again, and this second time there must be no failure. Even if he succeeded, he would most likely lose some toes. His feet must be badly frozen by now, and there would be some time before the second fire was ready.

Such were his thoughts, but he did not sit and think them. He was busy all the time they were passing through his mind. He made a new foundation for a fire, this time in the open, where no treacherous tree could blot it out. Next, he gathered dry grasses and tiny twigs from the high-water flotsam. He could not bring his fingers together to pull them out, but he was able to gather them by the handful. In this way he got many rotten twigs and bits of green moss that were undesirable, but it was the best he could do. He worked methodically, even collecting an armful of the larger branches to be used later when the fire gathered strength. And all the while the dog sat and watched him, a certain yearning wistfulness in its eyes, for it looked upon him as the fire-provider, and the fire was slow in coming.

When all was ready, the man reached in his pocket for a second piece of birch-bark. He knew the bark was there, and, though he could not feel it with his fingers, he could hear its crisp rustling as he fumbled for it. Try as he would, he could not clutch hold of it. And all the time, in his consciousness, was the knowledge that each instant his feet were freezing. This thought tended to put him in a panic, but he fought against it and kept calm.

He stripped the mitten from his right hand and fetched forth the birch-bark. The exposed fingers were quickly going numb again. Next he brought out his bunch of sulphur matches. But the tremendous cold had already driven the life out of his fingers. In his effort to separate one match from the others, the whole bunch fell in the snow. He tried to pick it out of the snow, but failed. The dead fingers could neither touch nor clutch. He was very careful.

He succeeded in getting one, which he dropped on his lap. He was no better off. He could not pick it up. Then he devised a way. He picked it up in his teeth and scratched it on his leg. Twenty times he scratched before he succeeded in lighting it. As it flamed he held it with his teeth to the birch-bark. But the burning brimstone went up his nostrils and into his lungs, causing him to cough spasmodically. The match fell into the snow and went out.

At last, when he could endure no more, he jerked his hands apart. The blazing matches fell sizzling into the snow, but the birch-bark was alight. He began laying dry grasses and the tiniest twigs on the flame. He could not pick and choose, for he had to lift the fuel between the heels of his hands. Small pieces of rotten wood and green moss clung to the twigs, and he bit them off as well as he could with his teeth. He cherished the flame carefully and awkwardly. It meant life, and it must not perish. The withdrawal of blood from the surface of his body now made him begin to shiver, and he grew more awkward. A large piece of green moss fell squarely on the little fire.

He tried to poke it out with his fingers, but his shivering frame made him poke too far, and he disrupted the nucleus of the little fire, the burning grasses and tiny twigs separating and scattering. He tried to poke them together again, but in spite of the tenseness of the effort, his shivering got away with him, and the twigs were hopelessly scattered. Each twig gushed a puff of smoke and went out. The fire-provider had failed. As he looked apathetically about him, his eyes chanced on the dog, sitting across the ruins of the fire from him, in the snow, making restless, hunching movements, slightly lifting one forefoot and then the other, shifting its weight back and forth on them with wistful eagerness.

The sight of the dog put a wild idea into his head. He remembered the tale of the man, caught in a blizzard, who killed a steer and crawled inside the carcass, and so was saved. He would kill the dog and bury his hands in the warm body until the numbness went out of them. Then he could build another fire. He spoke to the dog, calling it to him; but in his voice was a strange note of fear that frightened the animal, who had never known the man to speak in such way before. Something was the matter, and its suspicious nature sensed danger--it knew not what danger, but somewhere, somehow, in its brain arose an apprehension of the man. It flattened its ears down at the sound of the man's voice, and its restless, hunching movements and the lifting and shifting of its forefeet became more pronounced; but it would not come to the man. He got on his hands and knees and crawled toward the dog. This unusual posture again excited suspicion, and the animal sidled mincingly away.

But it was all he could do, hold its body encircled in his arms and sit there. He realized that he could not kill the dog. There was no way to do it. With his helps hands he could neither draw nor hold his sheath-knife nor throttle the animal. He released it, and it plunged wildly away, with tail between its legs, and still snarling. It halted forty feet away and surveyed him curiously, with ears sharply pricked forward.

A certain fear of death, dull and oppressive, came to him. This fear quickly became poignant as he realized that it was no longer a mere matter of freezing his fingers and toes, or of losing his hands and feet, but that it was a matter of life and death with the chances against him. This threw him into a panic, and he turned and ran up the creek-bed along the old, dim trail. The dog joined in behind and kept up with him. He ran blindly, without intention, in fear such as he had never known in his life…

It struck him as curious that he could run at all on feet so frozen that he could not feel them when they struck the earth and took the weight of his body. He seemed to himself to skim along above the surface, and to have no connection with the earth. Somewhere he had once seen a winged Mercury, and he wondered if Mercury felt as he felt when skimming over the earth.

His theory of running until he reached camp and the boys had one flaw in it: he lacked the endurance. Several times he stumbled, and finally he tottered, crumpled up, and fell. When he tried to rise, he failed. He must sit and rest, he decided, and next time he would merely walk and keep on going. As he sat and regained his breath, he noted that he was feeling quite warm and comfortable. He was not shivering, and it even seemed that a warm glow had come to his chest and trunk. And yet, when he touched his nose or cheeks, there was no sensation. Running would not thaw them out. Nor would it thaw out his hands and feet. Then the thought came to him that the frozen portions of his body must be extending. He tried to keep this thought down, to forget it, to think of something else; he was aware of the panicky feeling that it caused, and he was afraid of the panic. But the thought asserted itself, and persisted, until it produced a vision of his body totally frozen. This was too much, and he made another wild run along the trail. Once he slowed down to a walk, but the thought of the freezing extending itself made him run again.

And all the time the dog ran with him, at his heels. When he fell down a second time, it curled its tail over its forefeet and sat in front of him, facing him, curiously eager and intent. The warmth and security of the animal angered him, and he cursed it till it flattened down its ears appeasingly. This time the shivering came more quickly upon the man. He was losing in his battle with the frost. It was creeping into his body from all sides. The thought of it drove him on, but he ran no more than a hundred feet, when he staggered and pitched headlong. It was his last panic. When he had recovered his breath and control, he sat up and entertained in his mind the conception of meeting death with dignity. However, the conception did not come to him in such terms. His idea of it was that he had been making a fool of himself, running around like a chicken with its head cut off--such was the simile that occurred to him. Well, he was bound to freeze anyway, and he might as well take it decently. With this new-found peace of mind came the first glimmerings of drowsiness. A good idea, he thought, to sleep off to death. It was like taking an anaesthetic. Freezing was not so bad as people thought. There were lots worse ways to die.

He pictured the boys finding his body next day. Suddenly he found himself with them, coming along the trail and looking for himself. And, still with them, he came around a turn in the trail and found himself lying in the snow. He did not belong with himself any more, for even then he was out of himself, standing with the boys and looking at himself in the snow. It certainly was cold, was his thought. When he got back to the States he could tell the folks what real cold was. He drifted on from this to a vision of the old-timer on Sulphur Creek. He could see him quite clearly, warm and comfortable, and smoking a pipe.

"You were right, old hoss; you were right," the man mumbled to the old-timer of Sulphur Creek.

Then the man drowsed off into what seemed to him the most comfortable and satisfying sleep he had ever known. The dog sat facing him and waiting. The brief day drew to a close in a long, slow twilight. There were no signs of a fire to be made, and, besides, never in the dog's experience had it known a man to sit like that in the snow and make no fire. As the twilight drew on, its eager yearning for the fire mastered it, and with a great lifting and shifting of forefeet, it whined softly, then flattened its ears down in anticipation of being chidden by the man. But the man remained silent. Later, the dog whined loudly. And still later it crept close to the man and caught the scent of death. This made the animal bristle and back away. A little longer it delayed, howling under the stars that leaped and danced and shone brightly in the cold sky. Then it turned and trotted up the trail in the direction of the camp it knew, where were the other food-providers and fire-providers.

-End

8 史蒂芬・克蘭《海上扁舟》
——怒海中的人性光輝

小說特徵

寫實主義、自然主義與印象派的結合

史蒂芬・克蘭
（Stephen Crane, 1871-1900）

Stephen Crane's fiction presents a "symbiosis" of Naturalistic ideals and Impressionistic methods…a story should be logical in its action and faithful to character. Truth to life itself was the only test, the greatest artists were the simplest, and simple because they were true.

-Critic Sergio Perosa

史蒂芬・克蘭小說呈現是一自然主義理想與印象派方法的合成。……小說應該行為合理，忠實於角色；惟一標準就是生活的真實感，最偉大的藝術家都是最單純的，因為簡單就是真實。

——評論家　塞吉歐・培洛沙

作者短評

　　史蒂芬・克蘭（Stephen Crane），1871年，出生於美國新澤西州，自幼多病，父親是衛理公會（Methodist）牧師，史蒂芬克蘭四歲即能提筆寫作，先就讀Claverack軍校，雖不能順利適應而離開，這段時光卻讓從沒戰爭經驗的克蘭，為他日後勝任戰地記者與創作戰爭小說上，提供了極大幫助。

　　史蒂芬・克蘭，之後，在拉法葉學院（Lafayette College）及雪城大學（Syracuse University）各讀了一年書，進入報社工作。1892年，因報導有關工人罷工事件，遭報社解僱。1893年，史蒂芬・克蘭在紐約只好擔任自由新聞記者（free lancer）討生活，他根據報紙上的報導，深入貧民窟採訪，寫成了他的第一本小說《梅姬：一個阻街女郎》，克蘭抱持悲觀的宿命傾向，講述了女主角梅姬因被愛人所陷，成為妓女的悲慘境遇，雖出污泥不染，卻不敵現實環境犧牲的故事，被讚譽是美國有關貧民窟最寫實小說。1894年發表小說《紅色英勇勳章》（*The Red Badge of Courage*），以美國內戰為內容，描述戰場心理與恐怖之逼真，讓人有如親臨現場，樹立了他在美國文壇上不可動搖的地位。

　　1896年，史蒂芬・克蘭因幫兩名妓女作偽證，官司鬧得沸沸揚揚，全國矚目下，使他聲名大損，此時美國擴張主義正盛，極欲吞併古巴，與西班牙關係已到一觸即發的戰爭邊緣，趁此，史蒂芬・克蘭接受報社的邀約，改換跑道，當上

了戰地記者，首件差使，正是前往古巴採訪，在佛羅里達州的
Jacksonville等船期間，也結識日後不離不棄、梅開二渡，三十一
歲的柯拉‧泰勒（Cora Taylor），這大概是他人生最後一件所遇
幸運之事。1897年1月1日終於搭上 *SS Commodore* 汽船出海，大霧
中觸礁，棄船逃生，在海上漂流30小時後，終於得救上岸。史
蒂芬克蘭就是根據這次經歷，寫成短篇小說《海上扁舟》（*The
Open Boat*），細緻地描寫了四人如何在茫茫大海中掙扎與求生的
過程，是美國最著名短篇小說之一。

　　1898年，美、西為爭奪古巴開戰，克蘭再次去古巴採訪美
西戰爭。由於史蒂芬‧克蘭自《紅色英勇勳章》後，接續作品
銷路不佳，在美國文壇咸認是江郎才盡之下，克蘭與柯拉移居
英國發展寫作生涯，依不見起色，加上健康與財務困擾不斷，
1900年，肺病過逝，年僅二十九歲。

作品分析

　　相較畢爾斯以戰爭及傑克‧倫敦以「北國」為背景的寫
實題材，史蒂芬‧克蘭兩者兼具，三人可說是最具美國自然主
義特色及代表的小說家。克蘭的《紅色英勇勳章》、《梅姬：
一個阻街女郎》與所選短篇小說《海上扁舟》，主角不論是在
貧民窟、戰場與大海環境，都採取自然主義作品方式，將主
角個人獨立於社會、上帝及自然之上，身陷在生與死、理想與
現實、勇氣與怯懦及信心與恐懼的對立之間，沒有浪漫的樂觀
主義，只有人性的堅韌與脆弱，簡單呈現人心惟危時的赤裸呈

現；惟史蒂芬克蘭運用自然主義，描寫一個人對環境的反應時，似乎更多了一份強調在人性恐懼時，所透露出那一絲可貴的人性光輝，這在他《梅姬：一個阻街女郎》寫道：

> 您不可避免地要被這本書極大地震驚。但是請往下讀，鼓起所有的勇氣讀到最後一頁，因為這本書表明，環境在這個世界上舉足輕重，它往往毫不留情地塑造人們的生活。如果誰能證實這條理論，他就能為所有的靈魂在天堂裡找到一席之地（即便是一個偶然失足的街頭女郎）。

《海上扁舟》中，也充滿四人的扶持互助克服海上漂流時一再遭遇的失望與無助。

史蒂芬・克蘭作品除具備自然與寫實的特徵外，另外就是他習慣在小說中，對景色的光線與明暗的描寫，就像是印象主義畫家一般，試圖以精確渲染的場景作為一個整體，利用生動活潑的色彩及形象而聞名，在《海上扁舟》中，一開頭：「已沒有人知道天空的顏色。他們的眼光都平坦鎖定不斷向他們襲來的海浪，除了浪端的泡沫白色，海浪已像是調色盤一般，他們對大海的顏色已是瞭如指掌。」，克蘭習慣性描繪光景的內容，隨處可見。

The Open Boat

by Stephen Crane

I

None of them knew the color of the sky. Their eyes glanced level, and were fastened upon the waves that swept toward them…These waves were abrupt and tall, and each froth-top was a problem in small-boat navigation.

The cook squatted in the bottom and looked with both eyes at the six inches of gunwale which separated him from the ocean.

The oiler, steering with one of the two oars in the boat, sometimes raised himself suddenly to keep clear of water that swirled in over the stern. It was a thin little oar and it seemed often ready to snap.

The correspondent, pulling at the other oar, watched the waves and wondered why he was there.

The injured captain, lying in the bow, was at this time buried in that profound dejection and indifference…

"Keep 'er a little more south, Billie," said he.

"'A little more south,' sir," said the oiler in the stern.

II

As the boat bounced from the top of each wave, the wind tore through the hair of the hatless men, and as the craft plopped her stern down again the spray splashed past them. The crest of each of these waves was a hill, from the top of which the men surveyed, for a moment, a broad tumultuous expanse, shining and wind-riven. It was probably splendid. It was probably glorious, this play of the free sea, wild with lights of emerald and white and amber.

"Bully good thing it's an on-shore wind," said the cook.

"That's right," said the correspondent.

The busy oiler nodded his assent.

Then the captain, in the bow, chuckled in a way that expressed humor, contempt, tragedy, all in one.

"Oh, well," said the captain, soothing his children, "We'll get ashore all right."

In the meantime the oiler and the correspondent rowed. And also they rowed.

"See it?" said the captain.

"No," said the correspondent slowly, "I didn't see anything."

"Look again," said the captain. He pointed. "It's exactly in that direction."

At the top of another wave, the correspondent did as he was bid, and this time his eyes chanced on a small still thing on the edge of the swaying horizon. It was precisely like the point of a pin. It took an anxious eye to find a light house so tiny.

"Think we'll make it, captain?"

"If this wind holds and the boat don't swamp, we can't do much else," said the captain.

The little boat, lifted by each towering sea, and splashed viciously by the crests, made progress that in the absence of seaweed was not apparent to those in her. She seemed just a wee thing wallowing, miraculously top-up, at the mercy of five oceans. Occasionally, a great spread of water, like white flames, swarmed into her.

"Bail her, cook," said the captain serenely.

"All right, captain," said the cheerful cook.

III

It would be difficult to describe the subtle brotherhood of men that was here established on the seas. No one said that it was so. No one mentioned it. But it dwelt in the boat, and each man felt it warm him. They were a captain, an oiler, a cook, and a correspondent, and they were friends, friends in a more curiously iron-bound degree than may be common. The hurt captain, lying against the water-jar in the bow, spoke always in a low voice and calmly, but he could never command a more ready and swiftly obedient crew than the motley three of the dingey. It was more than a mere recognition of what was best for the common safety. There was surely in it a quality that was personal and heartfelt. And after this devotion to the commander of the boat there was this comradeship that the correspondent, for instance, who had been taught to be cynical of men, knew even at the time was the best experience of his life. But no one said that it was so. No one mentioned it.

Meanwhile the lighthouse had been growing slowly larger. It had now almost assumed color, and appeared like a little grey shadow on the sky. The man at the oars could not be prevented from turning his head rather often to try for a glimpse of this little grey shadow.

"Take her easy, now, boys," said the captain. "Don't spend yourselves. If we have to run a surf you'll need all your strength, because we'll sure have to swim for it. Take your time."

Slowly the land arose from the sea. From a black line it became a line of black and a line of white, trees and sand. Finally, the captain said that he could make out a house on the shore. "That's the house of refuge, sure," said the cook. "They'll see us before long, and come out after us."

The distant lighthouse reared high. "The keeper ought to be able to make us out now, if he's looking through a glass," said the captain. "He'll notify the life-saving people."

... the little boat turned her nose once more down the wind, and all but the oarsman watched the shore grow. The management of the boat was still most absorbing, but it could not prevent a quiet cheerfulness. In an hour, perhaps, they would be ashore.

The correspondent thought that he had been drenched to the skin, but happening to feel in the top pocket of his coat, he found therein eight cigars. After a search, somebody produced three dry matches, and with an assurance of an impending rescue shining in their eyes, puffed at the big cigars and judged well and ill of all men. Everybody took a drink of water.

IV

"Cook," remarked the captain, "there don't seem to be any signs of life about your house of refuge."

"No," replied the cook. "Funny they don't see us!"

"Funny they don't see us."

The lightheartedness of a former time had completely faded. To their sharpened minds it was easy to conjure pictures of all kinds of incompetency and blindness and, indeed, cowardice. There was the shore of the populous land, and it was bitter and bitter to them that from it came no sign.

"Well," said the captain, ultimately, "I suppose we'll have to make a try for ourselves. If we stay out here too long, we'll none of us have strength left to swim after the boat swamps."

And so the oiler, who was at the oars, turned the boat straight for the shore. There was a sudden tightening of muscle. There was some thinking.

"If we don't all get ashore--" said the captain. "If we don't all get ashore, I suppose you fellows know where to send news of my finish?"

They then briefly exchanged some addresses and admonitions. As for the reflections of the men, there was a great deal of rage in them.

The billows that came at this time were more formidable.

There was a considerable silence as the boat bumped over the furrowed sea to deeper water. Then somebody in gloom spoke. "Well, anyhow, they must have seen us from the shore by now."

The gulls went in slanting flight up the wind toward the grey desolate east. A squall, marked by dingy clouds, and clouds brick-red, like smoke from a burning building, appeared from the south-east.

"What do you think of those life-saving people? Ain't they peaches?'

"Funny they haven't seen us."

"Maybe they think we're out here for sport! Maybe they think we're fishin'. Maybe they think we're damned fools."

"Look! There's a man on the shore!"

"Where?"

"There! See 'im? See 'im?"

"Yes, sure! He's walking along."

"Now he's stopped. Look! He's facing us!"

"He's waving at us!"

"So he is! By thunder!"

"Ah, now we're all right! Now we're all right! There'll be a boat out here for us in half-an-hour."

"He's going on. He's running. He's going up to that house there."

"What's he doing now?"

"He's standing still again. He's looking, I think...There he goes again. Toward the house...Now he's stopped again."

"Is he waving at us?"

"No, not now! he was, though."

"Look! There comes another man!"

"That's it, likely. Look! There's a fellow waving a little black flag.

"That ain't a flag, is it? That's his coat. Why, certainly, that's his coat."

"What's that idiot with the coat mean? What's he signaling, anyhow?"

"It looks as if he were trying to tell us to go north. There must be a life-saving station up there."

"No! He thinks we're fishing."

"Well, I wish I could make something out of those signals. What do you suppose he means?"

"He don't mean anything. He's just playing."

The shore grew dusky. The man waving a coat blended gradually into this gloom, and it swallowed in the same manner the omnibus and the group of people.

This was surely a quiet evening. All save the oarsman lay heavily and listlessly in the boat's bottom. As for him, his eyes were just capable of noting the tall black waves that swept forward in a most sinister silence, save for an occasional subdued growl of a crest.

The cook's head was on a thwart, and he looked without interest at the water under his nose. He was deep in other scenes. Finally he spoke. "Billie," he murmured, dreamfully, "what kind of pie do you like best?"

"Pie," said the oiler and the correspondent, agitatedly. "Don't talk about those things, blast you!"

"Well," said the cook, "I was just thinking about ham sandwiches, and--"

V

When it occurs to a man that nature does not regard him as

important, and that she feels she would not maim the universe by disposing of him, he at first wishes to throw bricks at the temple, and he hates deeply the fact that there are no brick and no temples. Any visible expression of nature would surely be pelleted with his jeers.

The captain, in the bow, moved on his water-jar and sat erect. "Pretty long night," he observed to the correspondent. He looked at the shore.

"Those life-saving people take their time."

"Did you see that shark playing around?"

"Yes, I saw him. He was a big fellow, all right."

"Wish I had known you were awake."

Later the correspondent spoke into the bottom of the boat.

"Billie!" There was a slow and gradual disentanglement. "Billie, will you spell me?"

"Sure," said the oiler.

VI

When the correspondent again opened his eyes, the sea and the sky were each of the grey hue of the dawning. Later, carmine and gold was painted upon the waters. The morning appeared finally, in its splendor, with a sky of pure blue, and the sunlight flamed on the tips of the waves.

"Now, boys," said the captain, "she is going to swamp, sure. All we can do is to work her in as far as possible, and then when she swamps, pile out and scramble for the beach. Keep cool now, and don't jump until she swamps sure."

The monstrous in-shore rollers heaved the boat high until the men were again enabled to see the white sheets of water scudding up the slanted beach.

There were no hurried words, no pallor, no plain agitation. The men simply looked at the shore. "Now, remember to get well clear of the boat when you jump," said the captain.

"Steady now," said the captain. The men were silent...

But the next crest crashed also. The tumbling, boiling flood of white water caught the boat and whirled it almost perpendicular. Water swarmed in from all sides...The little boat, drunken with this weight of water, reeled and snuggled deeper into the sea.

"Bail her out, cook! Bail her out," said the captain.

"All right, captain," said the cook.

"Now, boys, the next one will do for us, sure," said the oiler. "Mind to jump clear of the boat."

The third wave moved forward, huge, furious, implacable. It fairly swallowed the dingey, and almost simultaneously the men tumbled into the sea. A piece of lifebelt had lain in the bottom of the boat, and as the correspondent went overboard he held this to his chest with his left hand.

In his struggle to reach the captain and the boat, he reflected that when one gets properly wearied, drowning must really be a comfortable arrangement, a cessation of hostilities accompanied by a large degree of relief, and he was glad of it, for the main thing in his mind for some months had been horror of the temporary agony. He did not wish to be hurt.

Presently he saw a man running along the shore. He was undressing with most remarkable speed. Coat, trousers, shirt, everything flew magically off him.

"Come to the boat," called the captain.

"All right, captain." As the correspondent paddled, he saw the captain let himself down to bottom and leave the boat. Then the correspondent performed his one little marvel of the voyage. A large wave caught him and flung him with ease and supreme speed completely over the boat and far beyond it. It struck him even then as an event in gymnastics, and a true miracle of the sea. An over-turned boat in the surf is not a plaything to a swimming man.

The correspondent arrived in water that reached only to his waist, but his condition did not enable him to stand for more than a moment. Each wave knocked him into a heap, and the under-tow pulled at him.

Then he saw the man who had been running and undressing, and undressing and running, come bounding into the water. He dragged ashore the cook, and then waded towards the captain, but the captain waved him away, and sent him to the correspondent. He was naked, naked as a tree in winter, but a halo was about his head, and he shone like a saint. He gave a strong pull, and a long drag, and a bully heave at the correspondent's hand. The correspondent, schooled in the minor formulae, said: "Thanks, old man." But suddenly the man cried: "What's that?" He pointed a swift finger. The correspondent said: "Go."

In the shallows, face downward, lay the oiler. His forehead touched sand that was periodically, between each wave, clear of the sea.

The correspondent did not know all that transpired afterward. When he achieved safe ground he fell, striking the sand with each particular part of his body. It was as if he had dropped from a roof, but the thud was grateful to him.

It seems that instantly the beach was populated with men with blankets, clothes, and flasks, and women with coffeepots and all the remedies sacred to their minds. The welcome of the land to the men from the sea was warm and generous, but a still and dripping shape was carried slowly up the beach, and the land's welcome for it could only be the different and sinister hospitality of the grave.

When it came night, the white waves paced to and fro in the moonlight, and the wind brought the sound of the great sea's voice to the men on shore, and they felt that they could then be interpreters.

海明威《白象似的群山》
——無聲勝有聲的弦外之音

小說特徵

「冰山理論」

（The Theory of Iceberg）

歐內斯特・海明威
（Ernest Hemingway, 1899-1961）

I always try to write on the principal of the iceberg .
There is seven-eights of it under water for every part that shows.
Anything you know you can eliminate and it only strengthens your iceberg.
It is the part that doesn't show.

-Ernest Hemingway

我總試著以「冰山原則」寫作。水下的部分占整座冰山的八分之七。凡是已知的，盡皆刪去；才足以強固你冰山下，那一隱藏的部分。

——海明威

作者短評

　　如果要挑選一位最能展現美國民族性格——粗獷、浪漫、坦率直接，不說廢話的小說家代表，給我海明威，其餘免談！

　　海明威（Ernest Miller Hemingway），1899年，出生於美國芝加哥市，家境富裕。海明威一生以戰爭、美人、醇酒為尚，與鬥牛、釣魚、狩獵為伍，身型魁梧偉岸，充滿男人陽剛形象，風流浪漫中，感情錯綜複雜，先後結過四次婚，是一次大戰後，美國「失落的一代」（the lost generation）狂歡、頹廢與迷茫、徬徨特質，最具鮮明形象的代表，而他豪邁與大膽的男性意識，無遺的表現在他作品之中，使戰爭與性愛成為他文學的兩大主題特色。

　　海明威視戰場為浪漫與英雄主義的聖地，每次爆發戰爭，他都不顧生死的奔赴戰場，《戰地春夢》即是他刻劃一次大戰所造成人類無可彌補的創傷，《戰地鐘聲》則以西班牙內戰為背景，二次大戰，海明威照樣參與，不落人後，堪稱是最Man的小說家。1954年《老人與海》，敘述一個老漁民捕獵到一條大馬林魚，但是後來被鯊魚吃掉的故事，為他贏得了諾貝爾文學獎。

　　海明威除在戰爭的暴力中，尋找英雄浪漫，激勵人道精神外，性愛與性別是他另一個極其曖昧的小說主題；文中常現柔順甜美、面目模糊的女子且地處弱勢，如男性的附屬，這在《白象似的群山》中男主角希望女主角墮胎或《戰地春夢》中女主角凱薩琳勇於當未婚媽媽，故事最後安排難產、母子皆死的結局，似乎也是反射海明威沉湎於性愛歡樂，不願當父親的性格寫照。

海明威的寫作風格以簡潔著稱，對美國文學及二十世紀文學的發展有極深遠的影響；最足具體代表者，莫過他所提出「冰山原則」已是小說創作與欣賞之圭臬，海明威創作《老人與海》時，就嘗試把一切不必要向讀者傳達的內容信息都統統刪除，只突出人物和故事情節，因此，他把社會背景淡化了，而更加側重於人物的內心獨白和動作，其他人物，都是淡淡幾筆勾勒其模糊的形象，給人朦朦朧朧的感覺。簡白式的文體吸引了大批仿效者，掀起了小說寫作上的臨摹風潮，固然，這與他記者出身，所受要簡不繁的文筆訓練大有關係，但文如其人，更是他愛恨分明，感情直接的性格寫照。1961年7月2日，海明威久病厭世，在家中以獵槍自殺身亡。

作品分析

海明威提出小說對白之「冰山理論」（The Theory of Iceberg），也就是以最簡約的話語，聚隱最深邃的能量，使小說中對白的運用，有如冰山在水面上的小露，卻隱約暗示了水面下積蘊的巨大能量，也是這股「無聲勝有聲，弦外之音」的想像奧妙，讓讀者更即溶於水面下的深邃，史考特・費茲傑羅（F. Scott Fitzgerald）讚美「所有好的寫作都是暗潮洶湧，令你屏息以待。」（All good writing is swimming under water and holding your breath.）

足堪表現這一「無聲勝有聲」理論，海明威的小說《白象似的群山》公論是典範之作，文中人物沒有確切的身份，沒有外貌，故事也沒有歷史時間，可是讀者不會感到話題的陌生，沒有感到消化閱讀的困難。一開場，女人以一座如白象的山脈，撩起話題，男人則心不在焉，一心一意只想勸女孩答應墮胎。兩人攻防之間衝突，自此，一直都是有形無形地的存在著；許多次一來一往間，言不及義的對話，像各自佈局的心理戰。我們當然明白，表面上佔上風的看來是女子，但是私下操縱全局的仍是她的男人。男人策略總是一切以「為她著想」的哄騙，讓女人甘心接受「手術」（是全文最接近墮胎的字眼），對話中，男人威逼利誘、不負責任的逃避心態表現無遺，讓人為女主角的卑微更加不捨，女子無奈、鬱悶及絕望，終於在憤怒中爆發，吶喊著：

"Would you please please please please please please please stop talking."

中宣洩殆盡時，轉念之間，女子最後也只能屈服男人的陽剛，悲愴以：

"There's nothing wrong with me. I feel fine."

話下結局，強顏歡笑將眼前的苦酒與悲傷，一飲而盡，道盡女子在愛人、墮胎兩難間的委曲求全。全篇欲蓋彌彰，張力十足的交鋒對話，讓你不得不佩服海明威簡單有力的心靈震撼！

Hills Like White Elephants

by Ernest Hemingway

The hills across the valley of the Ebro were long and white. On this side there was no shade and no trees and the station was between two lines of rails in the sun. Close against the side of the station there was the warm shadow of the building and a curtain, made of strings of bamboo beads, hung across the open door into the bar, to keep out flies. The American and the girl with him sat at a table in the shade, outside the building. It was very hot and the express from Barcelona would come in forty minutes. It stopped at this junction for two minutes and went on to Madrid. "What should we drink?" the girl asked. She had taken off her hat and put it on the table. "It's pretty hot," the man said. "Let's drink beer." " Dos cervezas," the man said into the curtain. "Big ones?" a woman asked from the doorway. "Yes. Two big ones." The woman brought two glasses of beer and two felt pads. She put the felt pads and the beer glasses on the table and looked at the man and the girl. The girl was looking off at the line of hills. They were white in the sun and the country was brown and dry.

"They look like white elephants," she said.

"I've never seen one," the man drank his beer.

"No, you wouldn't have."

"I might have," the man said, just because you say I wouldn't have doesn't prove anything."

The girl looked at the bead curtain.

"They've painted something on it," she said.

"What does it say?"

"Anis del Toro. It's a drink."

"Could we try it?"

The man called "Listen" through the curtain. The woman came out from the bar.

"We want two Anis del Toro."

"With water? "

"Do you want it with water?"

"I don't know," the girl said. "Is it good with water?" "It's all right."

"You want them with water?" asked the woman.

"Yes, with water."

"It tastes like licorice," the girl said and put the glass down.

"That's the way with everything."

"Yes," said the girl. "Everything tastes of licorice. Especially all the things you've waited so long for, like absinthe."

"Oh, cut it out."

"You started it," the girl said.

"I was being amused. I was having a fine time."

"Well, let's try and have a fine time."

"All right. I was trying. I said the mountains looked like white elephants. Wasn't that bright?"

"That was bright."

"I wanted to try this new drink. That's all we do, isn't it--look at things and try new drinks?"

"I guess so. "The girl looked across at the hills. "They're lovely hills," she said.

"They don't really look like white elephants. I just meant the coloring of their skin through the trees."

"Should we have another drink?"

"All right."

The warm wind blew the bead curtain against the table.

"The beer's nice and cool," the man said.

"It's lovely," the girl said.

"It's really an awfully simple operation, Jig," the man said.

"It's not really an operation at all. "The girl looked at the ground the table legs rested on.

"I know you wouldn't mind it, Jig. It's really not anything. It's just to let the air in. "The girl did not say anything. "I'll go with you and I'll stay with you all the time. They just let the air in and then it's all perfectly natural."

"Then what will we do afterward?"

"We'll be fine afterward. Just like we were before."

"What makes you think so?"

"That's the only thing that bothers us. It's the only thing that's made us unhappy. "

The girl looked at the bead curtain, put her hand out and took hold of two of the strings of beads.

" And you think then we'll be all right and be happy."

"I know we will. You don't have to be afraid. I've known lots of people that have done it."

"So have I," said the girl. "And afterward they were all so happy." "Well," the man said, "if you don't want to you don't have to. I wouldn't have you do it if you didn't want to. But I know it's perfectly simple." "And you really want to?" "I think it's the best thing to do. But I don't want you to do it if you don't really want to."

"And if I do it you'll be happy and things will be like they were and you'll love me?" "I love you now. You know I love you."

"I know. But if I do it, then it will be nice again if I say things are like white elephants, and you'll like it?"

"I'll love it. I love it now but I just can't think about it. You know how I get when I worry."

"If I do it you won't ever worry?"

"I won't worry about that because it's perfectly simple."

"Then I'll do it. Because I don't care about me."

"What do you mean?" "I don't care about me."

"Well, I care about you." "Oh, yes. But I don't care about me. And I'll do it and then everything will be fine."

"I don't want you to do it if you feel that way."

The girl stood up and walked to the end of the station. Across, on the other side, were fields of grain and trees along the banks of the Ebro. Far away, beyond the river, were mountains. The shadow of a cloud moved across the field of grain and she saw the river through the trees. "And we could have all this," she said. "And we could have everything and every day we make it more impossible."

"What did you say?"

"I said we could have everything." "We can have everything."

"No, we can't."

"We can have the whole world."

"No, we can't."

"We can go everywhere."

"No, we can't. It isn't ours any more."

"It's ours."

"No, it isn't. And once they take it away, you never get it back."

"But they haven't taken it away."

"We'll wait and see."

"Come on back in the shade," he said. "You mustn't feel that way."

"I don't feel any way," the girl said.

"I just know things." "I don't want you to do anything that you don't want to do "

"Nor that isn't good for me," she said.

"I know. Could we have another beer?"

"All right. But you've got to realize "

"I realize," the girl said. "Can't we maybe stop talking?"

They sat down at the table and the girl looked across at the hills on the dry side of the valley and them an looked at her and at the table. "You've got to realize," he said, "that I don't want you to do it if you don't want to. I'm perfectly willing to go through with it if it means anything to you."

"Doesn't it mean anything to you? We could get along."

"Of course it does. But I don't want anybody but you. I don't want any one else. And I know it's perfectly simple."

"Yes, you know it's perfectly simple."

"It's all right for you to say that, but I do know it."

"Would you do something for me now? "

" I'd do anything for you.'

" *Would you please please please please please please please Stop talking.*"

He did not say anything but looked at the bags against the wall of the station. There were labels on them from all the hotels where they had spent nights.

"But I don't want you to," he said,

"I don't care anything about it." "I'll scream," the girl said.

The woman came out through the curtains with two glasses of beer and put them down on the damp felt pads. "The train comes in five minutes," she said. "What did she say?" asked the girl. "That the train is coming in five minutes. "The girl smiled brightly at the woman, to thank her."I'd better take the bags over to the other side of the station," the man said. She smiled at him." All right. Then come back and we'll finish the beer. " He picked up the two heavy bags and carried them around the station to the other tracks. He looked up the tracks but could not see the train. Coming back, he walked through the barroom, where people waiting for the train were drinking. He drank an Anis at the bar and looked at the people. They were all waiting reasonably for the train. He went out through the bead curtain. She was sitting at the table and smiled at him.

"Do you feel better?" he asked.

"I feel fine," she said. "There's nothing wrong with me. I feel fine."

莫泊桑《項鍊》
——悲觀人生的戲謔大師

莫泊桑
(Guy de Maupassant, 1850-1893)

✒ 小說特徵

悲觀厭世、文筆戲謔、結局
意外

You see, human life, which is not people imagination of so good,
that's not so bad.

-Guy de Maupassant

你明白，人的一生，既不是人們想像的那麼好，也沒有那麼壞。

——莫泊桑

作者短評

　　莫泊桑（Guy de Maupassant），1850年，出生於法國西北部諾曼第，父親為一股票經紀人；母親獨立開明，喜愛文學，對經典作品如莎士比亞的戲劇深感興趣。十一歲時，父母離異，莫泊桑便一直和母親一起生活，受母影響甚深，是他一生最敬愛至親。莫泊桑一生未婚，持獨身主義，嘲謔婚姻「不過是白天交換惡劣的感情，晚上交換彼此的惡臭，如此而已」。莫泊桑是美國人最愛的外國作家，也深深影響美國小說家的寫作風格，如歐亨利。

　　莫泊桑十三歲時，開始寫詩，十七歲入天主教中學，卻痛恨宗教的形式與虛偽，嘲諷「宗教的目的就是填滿天國的金庫」，1870年莫泊桑畢業後不久，普法戰爭爆發，他勇敢志願入伍。戰後，他在海軍部門作了十年的公務員，在這十年單調生活中，他唯一的娛樂就是假日在塞納河上划船逍遙，卻也認識了大文豪福樓拜（Gustave Flaubert），福樓拜有如莫泊桑文學教父，指導莫泊桑的文學創作。在福樓拜家裡，莫泊桑遇到了屠格涅夫、左拉和都德等人，隨著短篇小說的發表和與名家交流，莫泊桑名氣日隆，他因寫作而名利雙收，出入巴黎的上流社會，但也縱情聲色、流連風月，後來染上梅毒。1880年完成了傑作《脂肪球》（Ball of Fat, 1880），獲得巨大成功，福樓拜稱之為「可以流傳於世的傑作」，他小說所反映出來的社會面十分寬廣，不管是哪一個階層的人物和生活，文中人物常抱持著悲觀厭世的氣氛，卻又以戲謔的態度揶揄，這般「憂鬱的浪漫主義」深得福樓拜真傳；情節的安排上更是細心照顧到讀者的閱讀興趣，他一生共寫了三百多篇短篇小說，享有「世界短篇小說之父」的美譽。

莫泊桑喜歡隱居與沉思，他常常獨自前往各地旅行尋找靈感。在1891年之後，莫泊桑越發喜歡孤獨的生活，最後他精神失常，經常擔心死亡與被迫害，加之他早年染上的梅毒，他感到非常痛苦，曾經試圖自殺。1893年過世於精神病院，得年四十三歲，墓碑上，刻道「我貪妄人生一切，卻不得樂趣」，一語道盡浮華放浪一生。

作品分析

《項鏈》是莫泊桑於1884年在法語報紙 *Le Gaulois* 上首次發表。該小說是莫泊桑最富盛名的作品之一，而莫泊桑扭曲式意外結尾的典型，也是日後美國小說家歐亨利與英國的毛姆所師承效仿。講述的是一位女子瑪蒂爾德，容貌姣美，身段窈窕，但出身貧窮，只好嫁給教育部的小科員，每天呆坐家中，想像著貴族的奢華生活。一天丈夫爭取到了供職教育部舉辦晚會的兩封請柬，丈夫把積蓄給她買了華麗的晚裝，衣服有了，可是首飾呢？因為沒有錢，丈夫讓她找她的好朋友珍妮借到了最眩目的寶石項鏈，也的確令她佔盡晚會的風頭，不料玩得太high，弄丟了項鏈。瑪蒂爾德和丈夫只好傾家蕩產，並借債湊齊三萬六千法郎買來新項鏈還給好朋友珍妮。隨後數年裡，她和丈夫省吃簡用，辛苦勞作，才償清債務。某日，瑪蒂爾德在街上偶遇珍妮，才知道好朋友珍妮原來的項鏈，只是價值五百法郎的假貨。

內容類似的作品也出現在莫泊桑的《珠寶》：朗丹先生一直認為自己很幸福，直到妻子過世，因意外發現妻子平日所收集的假珠寶竟然都是真的，進而也揭穿了所謂「幸福」的假象。結局的出奇與意外也構成莫泊桑短篇小說的極大特色與讀者期待的樂趣。

文選閱讀

The Necklace

by Guy de Maupassant

SHE WAS ONE OF THOSE PRETTY AND CHARMING GIRLS BORN, as though fate had blundered over her, into a family of artisans. She had no marriage portion, no expectations, no means of getting known, understood, loved, and wedded by a man of wealth and distinction; and she let herself be married off to a little clerk in the Ministry of Education. Her tastes were simple because she had never been able to afford any other, but she was as unhappy as though she had married beneath her; for women have no caste or class, their beauty, grace, and charm serving them for birth or family. Their natural delicacy, their instinctive elegance, their nimbleness of wit, are their only mark of rank, and put the slum girl on a level with the highest lady in the land.

She suffered endlessly, feeling herself born for every delicacy and luxury. She suffered from the poorness of her house, from its mean walls, worn chairs, and ugly curtains. All these things, of which other women of her class would not even have been aware, tormented and insulted her. The sight of the little Breton girl who came to do the work in her little house aroused heart-broken regrets and hopeless dreams in her mind. She imagined silent antechambers, heavy with Oriental tapestries, lit by torches in lofty bronze sockets, with two tall footmen in knee-breeches sleeping in large arm-chairs, overcome by the heavy warmth of the stove. She imagined vast saloons hung with antique silks, exquisite pieces of furniture supporting priceless ornaments, and small, charming, perfumed rooms, created just for little parties of intimate friends, men who were famous and sought after, whose homage roused every other woman's envious longings.

When she sat down for dinner at the round table covered with a three-days-old cloth, opposite her husband, who took the cover off the soup-tureen, exclaiming delightedly: "Aha! Scotch broth! What could be better?" she imagined delicate meals, gleaming silver, tapestries peopling the walls with folk of a past age and strange birds in faery forests; she imagined delicate food served in marvellous dishes, murmured gallantries, listened to with an inscrutable smile as one trifled with the rosy flesh of trout or wings of asparagus chicken.

She had no clothes, no jewels, nothing. And these were the only things she loved; she felt that she was made for them. She had longed so eagerly to charm, to be desired, to be wildly attractive and sought after.

She had a rich friend, an old school friend whom she refused to visit, because she suffered so keenly when she returned home. She would weep whole days, with grief, regret, despair, and misery.

One evening her husband came home with an exultant air, holding a large envelope in his hand.

" Here's something for you," he said.

Swiftly she tore the paper and drew out a printed card on which were these words:

"The Minister of Education and Madame Ramponneau request the pleasure of the company of Monsieur and Madame Loisel at the Ministry on the evening of Monday, January the 18th."

Instead of being delighted, as her-husband hoped, she flung the invitation petulantly across the table, murmuring:

"What do you want me to do with this?"

"Why, darling, I thought you'd be pleased. You never go out, and this is a great occasion. I had tremendous trouble to get it. Every one wants one; it's very select, and very few go to the clerks. You'll see all the really big people there."

She looked at him out of furious eyes, and said impatiently: "And what do you suppose I am to wear at such an affair?"

He had not thought about it; he stammered:

"Why, the dress you go to the theatre in. It looks very nice, to me..."

He stopped, stupefied and utterly at a loss when he saw that his wife was beginning to cry. Two large tears ran slowly down from the corners of her eyes towards the corners of her mouth.

"What's the matter with you? What's the matter with you?" he faltered.

But with a violent effort she overcame her grief and replied in a calm voice, wiping her wet cheeks:

"Nothing. Only I haven't a dress and so I can't go to this party. Give your invitation to some friend of yours whose wife will be turned out better than I shall."

He was heart-broken.

"Look here, Mathilde," he persisted. :What would be the cost of a suitable dress, which you could use on other occasions as well, something very simple?"

She thought for several seconds, reckoning up prices and also wondering for how large a sum she could ask without bringing upon herself an immediate refusal and an exclamation of horror from the careful-minded clerk.

At last she replied with some hesitation:

"I don't know exactly, but I think I could do it on four hundred francs."

He grew slightly pale, for this was exactly the amount he had been saving for a gun, intending to get a little shooting next summer on the plain of Nanterre with some friends who went lark-shooting there on Sundays.

Nevertheless he said: "Very well. I'll give you four hundred francs. But try and get a really nice dress with the money."

The day of the party drew near, and Madame Loisel seemed sad, uneasy and anxious. Her dress was ready, however. One evening her husband said to her:

"What's the matter with you? You've been very odd for the last three days."

"I'm utterly miserable at not having any jewels, not a single stone, to wear," she replied. "I shall look absolutely no one. I would almost rather not go to the party."

"Wear flowers," he said. "They're very smart at this time of the year. For ten francs you could get two or three gorgeous roses."

She was not convinced.

"No. .. there's nothing so humiliating as looking poor in the middle of a lot of rich women."

"How stupid you are!" exclaimed her husband. "Go and see Madame Forestier and ask her to lend you some jewels. You know her quite well enough for that."

She uttered a cry of delight.

"That's true. I never thought of it."

Next day she went to see her friend and told her her trouble.

Madame Forestier went to her dressing-table, took up a large box, brought it to Madame Loisel, opened it, and said:

"Choose, my dear."

First she saw some bracelets, then a pearl necklace, then a Venetian cross in gold and gems, of exquisite workmanship. She tried the effect of the jewels before the mirror, hesitating, unable to make up her mind to leave them, to give them up. She kept on asking:

"Haven't you anything else?"

"Yes. Look for yourself. I don't know what you would like best."

Suddenly she discovered, in a black satin case, a superb diamond necklace; her heart began to beat covetously. Her hands trembled as she lifted it. She fastened it round her neck, upon her high dress, and remained in ecstasy at sight of herself.

Then, with hesitation, she asked in anguish:

"Could you lend me this, just this alone?"

"Yes, of course."

She flung herself on her friend's breast, embraced her frenziedly, and went away with her treasure. The day of the party arrived. Madame Loisel was a success. She was the prettiest woman present, elegant, graceful, smiling, and quite above herself with happiness. All the men stared at her, inquired her name, and asked to be introduced to her. All the Under-Secretaries of State were eager to waltz with her. The Minister noticed her.

She danced madly, ecstatically, drunk with pleasure, with no thought for anything, in the triumph of her beauty, in the pride of her success, in a cloud of happiness made up of this universal homage and admiration, of the desires she had aroused, of the completeness of a victory so dear to her feminine heart.

She left about four o'clock in the morning. Since midnight her husband had been dozing in a deserted little room, in company with three other men whose wives were having a good time. He threw over her shoulders the garments he had brought for them to go home in, modest everyday clothes, whose poverty clashed with the beauty of the ball-dress. She was conscious of this and was anxious to hurry away, so that she should not be noticed by the other women putting on their costly furs.

Loisel restrained her.

"Wait a little. You'll catch cold in the open. I'm going to fetch a cab."

But she did not listen to him and rapidly descended-the staircase. When they were out in the street they could not find a cab; they began to look for one, shouting at the drivers whom they saw passing in the distance.

They walked down towards the Seine, desperate and shivering. At last they found on the quay one of those old nightprowling carriages which are only to be seen in Paris after dark, as though they were ashamed of their shabbiness in the daylight.

It brought them to their door in the Rue des Martyrs, and sadly they walked up to their own apartment. It was the end, for her. As for him, he was thinking that he must be at the office at ten.

She took off the garments in which she had wrapped her shoulders, so as to see herself in all her glory before the mirror. But suddenly she uttered a cry. The necklace was no longer round her neck!

"What's the matter with you?" asked her husband, already half undressed.

She turned towards him in the utmost distress.

"I... I... I've no longer got Madame Forestier's necklace..."

He started with astonishment.

"What!...Impossible!"

They searched in the folds of her dress, in the folds of the coat, in the pockets, everywhere. They could not find it.

"Are you sure that you still had it on when you came away from the ball?" he asked.

"Yes, I touched it in the hall at the Ministry."

"But if you had lost it in the street, we should have heard it fall."

"Yes. Probably we should. Did you take the number of the cab?"

"No. You didn't notice it, did you?"

"No."

They stared at one another, dumbfounded. At last Loisel put on his clothes again. "I'll go over all the ground we walked," he said, "and see if I can't find it." And he went out. She remained in her evening clothes, lacking strength to get into bed, huddled on a chair, without volition or power of thought. Her husband returned about seven. He had found nothing.

He went to the police station, to the newspapers, to offer a reward, to the cab companies, everywhere that a ray of hope impelled him.

She waited all day long, in the same state of bewilderment at this fearful catastrophe.

Loisel came home at night, his face lined and pale; he had discovered nothing.

"You must write to your friend," he said, "and tell her that you've broken the clasp of her necklace and are getting it mended. That will give us time to look about us."

She wrote at his dictation.

By the end of a week they had lost all hope.

Loisel, who had aged five years, declared:

"We must see about replacing the diamonds."

Next day they took the box which had held the necklace and went to the jewellers whose name was inside. He consulted his books.

"It was not I who sold this necklace, Madame; I must have merely supplied the clasp."

Then they went from jeweller to jeweller, searching for another necklace like the first, consulting their memories, both ill with remorse and anguish of mind.

In a shop at the Palais-Royal they found a string of diamonds which seemed to them exactly like the one they were looking for. It was worth forty thousand francs. They were allowed to have it for thirty-six thousand.

They begged the jeweller not to sell it for three days. And they arranged matters on the understanding that it would be taken back for thirty-four thousand francs, if the first one were found before the end of February.

Loisel possessed eighteen thousand francs left to him by his father. He intended to borrow the rest.

He did borrow it, getting a thousand from one man, five hundred from another, five louis here, three louis there. He gave notes of hand, entered into ruinous agreements, did business with usurers and the whole tribe of money-lenders. He mortgaged the whole remaining years of his existence, risked his signature without even knowing it he could honour it, and, appalled at the agonising face of the future, at the black misery about to fall upon him, at the prospect of every possible physical privation and moral torture, he went to get the new necklace and put down upon the jeweller's counter thirty-six thousand francs.

When Madame Loisel took back the necklace to Madame Forestier, the latter said to her in a chilly voice:

"You ought to have brought it back sooner; I might have needed it."

She did not, as her friend had feared, open the case. If she had noticed the substitution, what would she have thought? What would she have said? Would she not have taken her for a thief?

Madame Loisel came to know the ghastly life of abject poverty. From the very first she played her part heroically. This fearful debt must be paid off. She would pay it. The servant was dismissed. They changed their flat; they took a garret under the roof.

She came to know the heavy work of the house, the hateful duties of the kitchen. She washed the plates, wearing out her pink nails on the coarse pottery and the bottoms of pans. She washed the dirty linen, the shirts and dish-cloths, and hung them out to dry on a string; every morning she took the dustbin down into the street and carried up the water, stopping on each landing to get her breath. And, clad like a poor woman, she went to the fruiterer, to the grocer, to the butcher, a basket on her arm, haggling, insulted, fighting for every wretched halfpenny of her money.

Every month notes had to be paid off, others renewed, time gained. Her husband worked in the evenings at putting straight a merchant's accounts, and often at night he did copying at two pence-halfpenny a page. And this life lasted ten years.

At the end of ten years everything was paid off, everything, the usurer's charges and the accumulation of superimposed interest.

Madame Loisel looked old now. She had become like all the other strong, hard, coarse women of poor households. Her hair was badly done, her skirts were awry, her hands were red. She spoke in a shrill voice, and the water slopped all over the floor when she scrubbed it. But sometimes, when her husband was at the office, she sat down by the window and thought of that evening long ago, of the ball at which she had been so beautiful and so much admired.

What would have happened if she had never lost those jewels. Who knows? Who knows? How strange life is, how fickle! How little is needed to ruin or to save!

One Sunday, as she had gone for a walk along the Champs-Elysees to freshen herself after the labours of the week, she caught sight suddenly of a woman who was taking a child out for a walk. It was Madame Forestier, still young, still beautiful, still attractive.

Madame Loisel was conscious of some emotion. Should she speak to her? Yes, certainly. And now that she had paid, she would tell her all. Why not?

She went up to her.

"Good morning, Jeanne."

The other did not recognise her, and was surprised at being thus familiarly addressed by a poor woman.

"But...Madame..." she stammered. "I don't know... you must be making a mistake."

"No...I am Mathilde Loisel."

Her friend uttered a cry.

"Oh!...my poor Mathilde, how you have changed!..."

"Yes, I've had some hard times since I saw you last; and many sorrows...and all on your account."

"On my account!...How was that?"

"You remember the diamond necklace you lent me for the ball at the Ministry?"

"Yes. Well?"

"Well, I lost it."

"How could you? Why, you brought it back."

"I brought you another one just like it. And for the last ten years we have been paying for it. You realise it wasn't easy for us; we had no money...Well, it's paid for at last, and I'm glad indeed."

Madame Forestier had halted.

"You say you bought a diamond necklace to replace mine?"

"Yes. You hadn't noticed it? They were very much alike."

And she smiled in proud and innocent happiness.

Madame Forestier, deeply moved, took her two hands.

"Oh, my poor Mathilde! But mine was imitation. It was worth at the very most five hundred francs!

歐・亨利《最後一片葉子》
——短篇小說驚奇之王

小說特徵

「歐・亨利式結尾」
（O. Henry's twist）

歐・亨利
(O. Henry, 1862-1910)

*...and--look out the window at the last ivy leaf on the wall.
Didn't you wonder why it never fluttered or moved when the wind blew?
Ah, darling, it's Behrman's masterpiece--he painted it there the night
that the last leaf fell."*

-O. Henry, The Last Leaf

看著窗外攀爬在牆上的最後一片葉子。（蘇與喬安娜）不覺奇怪
這片葉子從不隨風飄揚或移動過？啊！親愛的，它是伯曼的傑
作，是那晚，當最後一片葉子落下時，他畫上的。

——歐・亨利《最後一片葉子》

作者短評

歐・亨利（O. Henry），1862年，出身於美國北卡羅來納州一個小鎮醫師家庭，原名威廉・西德尼・波特（William Sydney Porter），是美國最著名的短篇小說家之一，曾被評論界譽為美國現代短篇小說之父。

歐・亨利的一生富於傳奇性，當過藥房學徒、牛仔、會計員、土地辦事員、新聞記者、銀行出納員。當銀行出納員時，受疑挪用銀行現金，被捕入獄，獄中擔任醫務室的藥劑師時，開始認真寫作。獲釋後，1902年移居紐約，方改名歐・亨利，決心從事寫作專業。歐・亨利善於描寫美國社會，尤其是紐約百姓的生活，歐・亨利有很多的小說以紐約為背景，他筆下的紐約是個怪事層出不窮的大都市。

歐・亨利寫小說一心目的者乃「供讀者消遣」，他的作品構思新穎，幽默的語言始終貫穿，但結局絕對出人意外，讓人跌破眼鏡，這種出其不意，情節逆轉的結尾收場，成為了他小說中最大的特色，他「歐・亨利式結尾」（O. Henry's twist）據信深受莫泊桑小說的啟發而形成。

代表作有小說集《白菜與國王》、《四百萬》、《命運之路》等。其中一些名篇如《愛的犧牲》、《警察與讚美詩》、《帶傢具出租的房間》、《麥琪的禮物》、《最後一片葉子》等使他獲得了世界聲譽。

作品分析

　　小說寫作，搞神秘是最容易讓讀者上鉤的佈局，馬奎斯說過「每一篇好的小說都是這世界的一個謎」，但小說的引人入勝與否，則看最終謎題答案的揭曉方式。如果你喜歡享受Surprise或跌碎眼鏡的感覺，歐·亨利的短篇小說應該是不會使你失望的選擇。這歸功於他小說中最慣用和稱道的寫作策略——所謂「歐·亨利式結局」。

　　歐·亨利在每篇作品，當他開始慢慢鋪陳劇情的時候，總是利用讀者直線的思考方式，誤導歧途，同時底層早有一條細微的線索或精緻的伏筆隱藏其中，以至於當故事推展至最高潮時，筆鋒一轉，倏忽之間，總是以出人意料的結尾，畫下句點，讀者錯愕瞬間，往往先是出人意料，但經仔細一想，又會覺得其實合情合理，令人格外感到拍案叫絕，回味無窮。

　　歐·亨利幾乎在每一篇作品中都運用了這樣的寫作的佈局與技巧，讓讀者即使知道正面對一個說故事的「詐騙集團」，卻仍「甘心情願」期待享受被騙的驚奇。歐·亨利的小說世界如此充滿魅力，這也使得大多數人只要一談起歐·亨利的小說，立即浮現腦海的往往是某一篇故事裡的情節，而不是某一篇故事中的人物；他的「歐·亨利的結局」也早已成了一種文學創作模式，已是許多作家模仿的經典。

　　《最後一片葉子》是以紐約為背景，講述一群潦倒的藝術家彼此扶持的故事；畫家喬安娜生了病，失去求生意識，她看著窗外抵擋不過風雨的葉子，一片一片飄落，悲觀地倒數自己的生命。同時，樓下窮途潦倒，脾氣暴躁，吹噓要畫下一生傑作的老畫家伯曼，知道了這件事後，竟在風雨夜偷偷在牆頭畫上了一片永不掉落的葉子，鼓舞了喬安娜的求生意志，進而康復，伯曼卻因此染上急性肺炎死了。歐‧亨利以人道、幽默的深情筆觸，對社會底層的小人物予以特別關注，也將痛苦與幽默及悲慘與幸福，做了奇特混合，構成了他小說除驚奇之外，獨特擁有的人文關懷。

文選閱讀

The Last Leaf

by O. Henry

In a little district west of Washington Square the streets have run crazy and broken themselves into small strips called "places." These "places" make strange angles and curves. One Street crosses itself a time or two. An artist once discovered a valuable possibility in this street. Suppose a collector with a bill for paints, paper and canvas should, in traversing this route, suddenly meet himself coming back, without a cent having been paid on account!

So, to quaint old Greenwich Village the art people soon came prowling, hunting for north windows and eighteenth-century gables and

Dutch attics and low rents. Then they imported some pewter mugs and a chafing dish or two from Sixth Avenue, and became a "colony."

At the top of a squatty, three-story brick Sue and Johnsy had their studio. "Johnsy" was familiar for Joanna. One was from Maine; the other from California. They had met at the table d'hôte of an Eighth Street "Delmonico's," and found their tastes in art, chicory salad and bishop sleeves so congenial that the joint studio resulted.

That was in May. In November a cold, unseen stranger, whom the doctors called Pneumonia, stalked about the colony, touching one here and there with his icy fingers. Over on the east side this ravager strode boldly, smiting his victims by scores, but his feet trod slowly through the maze of the narrow and moss-grown "places."

Mr. Pneumonia was not what you would call a chivalric old gentleman. A mite of a little woman with blood thinned by California zephyrs was hardly fair game for the red-fisted, short-breathed old duffer. But Johnsy he smote; and she lay, scarcely moving, on her painted iron bedstead, looking through the small Dutch window-panes at the blank side of the next brick house.

One morning the busy doctor invited Sue into the hallway with a shaggy, gray eyebrow.

"She has one chance in--let us say, ten," he said, as he shook down the mercury in his clinical thermometer. "And that chance is for her to want to live. This way people have of lining-u on the side of the undertaker makes the entire pharmacopoeia look silly. Your little lady has made up her mind that she's not going to get well. Has she anything on her mind?"

"She--she wanted to paint the Bay of Naples some day." said Sue.

"Paint?--bosh! Has she anything on her mind worth thinking twice--a man for instance?"

"A man?" said Sue, with a jew's-harp twang in her voice. "Is a man worth--but, no, doctor; there is nothing of the kind."

"Well, it is the weakness, then," said the doctor. "I will do all that science, so far as it may filter through my efforts, can accomplish. But whenever my patient begins to count the carriages in her funeral procession I subtract 50 per cent from the curative power of medicines. If you will get her to ask one question about the new winter styles in cloak sleeves I will promise you a one-in-five chance for her, instead of one in ten."

After the doctor had gone Sue went into the workroom and cried a Japanese napkin to a pulp. Then she swaggered into Johnsy's room with her drawing board, whistling ragtime.

Johnsy lay, scarcely making a ripple under the bedclothes, with her face toward the window. Sue stopped whistling, thinking she was asleep.

She arranged her board and began a pen-and-ink drawing to illustrate a magazine story. Young artists must pave their way to Art by drawing pictures for magazine stories that young authors write to pave their way to Literature.

As Sue was sketching a pair of elegant horseshow riding trousers and a monocle of the figure of the hero, an Idaho cowboy, she heard a low sound, several times repeated. She went quickly to the bedside.

Johnsy's eyes were open wide. She was looking out the window and counting--counting backward.

"Twelve," she said, and little later "eleven"; and then "ten," and "nine"; and then "eight" and "seven", almost together.

Sue look solicitously out of the window. What was there to count? There was only a bare, dreary yard to be seen, and the blank side of the brick house twenty feet away. An old, old ivy vine, gnarled and decayed at the roots, climbed half way up the brick wall. The cold breath of autumn had stricken its leaves from the vine until its skeleton branches clung, almost bare, to the crumbling bricks.

"What is it, dear?" asked Sue.

"Six," said Johnsy, in almost a whisper. "They're falling faster now. Three days ago there were almost a hundred. It made my head ache to count them. But now it's easy. There goes another one. There are only five left now."

"Five what, dear? Tell your Sudie."

"Leaves. On the ivy vine. When the last one falls I must go, too. I've known that for three days. Didn't the doctor tell you?"

"Oh, I never heard of such nonsense," complained Sue, with magnificent scorn. "What have old ivy leaves to do with your getting well? And you used to love that vine so, you naughty girl. Don't be a goosey. Why, the doctor told me this morning that your chances for getting well real soon were--let's see exactly what he said--he said the chances were ten to one! Why, that's almost as good a chance as we have in New York when we ride on the street cars or walk past a new building. Try to take some broth now, and let Sudie go back to her drawing, so she can sell the editor man with it, and buy port wine for her sick child, and pork chops for her greedy self."

"You needn't get any more wine," said Johnsy, keeping her eyes fixed out the window. "There goes another. No, I don't want any broth. That leaves just four. I want to see the last one fall before it gets dark. Then I'll go, too."

"Johnsy, dear," said Sue, bending over her, "will you promise me to keep your eyes closed, and not look out the window until I am done working? I must hand those drawings in by to-morrow. I need the light, or I would draw the shade down."

"Couldn't you draw in the other room?" asked Johnsy, coldly.

"I'd rather be here by you," said Sue. "Beside, I don't want you to keep looking at those silly ivy leaves."

"Tell me as soon as you have finished," said Johnsy, closing her eyes, and lying white and still as fallen statue, "because I want to see the last one fall. I'm tired of waiting. I'm tired of thinking. I want to turn loose my hold on everything, and go sailing down, down, just like one of those poor, tired leaves."

"Try to sleep," said Sue. "I must call Behrman up to be my model for the old hermit miner. I'll not be gone a minute. Don't try to move 'til I come back."

Old Behrman was a painter who lived on the ground floor beneath them. He was past sixty and had a Michael Angelo's Moses beard curling down from the head of a satyr along with the body of an imp. Behrman was a failure in art. Forty years he had wielded the brush without getting near enough to touch the hem of his Mistress's robe. He had been always about to paint a masterpiece, but had never yet begun it. For several years he had painted nothing except now and then a daub in the line of commerce or advertising. He earned a little by serving as a model to those young artists in the colony who could not pay the price of a professional. He drank gin to excess, and still talked of his coming masterpiece. For the rest he was a fierce little old man, who scoffed terribly at softness in any one, and who regarded himself as especial mastiff-in-waiting to protect the two young artists in the studio above.

Sue found Behrman smelling strongly of juniper berries in his dimly lighted den below. In one corner was a blank canvas on an easel that had been waiting there for twenty-five years to receive the first line of the masterpiece. She told him of Johnsy's fancy, and how she feared she would, indeed, light and fragile as a leaf herself, float away, when her slight hold upon the world grew weaker.

Old Behrman, with his red eyes plainly streaming, shouted his contempt and derision for such idiotic imaginings.

"Vass!" he cried. "Is dere people in de world mit der foolishness to die because leafs dey drop off from a confounded vine? I haf not heard of such a thing. No, I will not bose as a model for your fool hermit-dunderhead. Vy do you allow dot silly pusiness to come in der brain of her? Ach, dot poor leetle Miss Yohnsy."

"She is very ill and weak," said Sue, "and the fever has left her mind morbid and full of strange fancies. Very well, Mr. Behrman, if you do not care to pose for me, you needn't. But I think you are a horrid old--old flibbertigibbet."

"You are just like a woman!" yelled Behrman. "Who said I will not bose? Go on. I come mit you. For half an hour I haf peen trying to say dot I am ready to bose. Gott! dis is not any blace in which one so goot as Miss Yohnsy shall lie sick. Some day I vill baint a masterpiece, and ve shall all go away. Gott! yes."

Johnsy was sleeping when they went upstairs. Sue pulled the shade down to the window-sill, and motioned Behrman into the other room. In there they peered out the window fearfully at the ivy vine. Then they looked at each other for a moment without speaking. A persistent, cold rain was falling, mingled with snow. Behrman, in his old blue shirt, took his seat as the hermit miner on an upturned kettle for a rock.

When Sue awoke from an hour's sleep the next morning she found Johnsy with dull, wide-open eyes staring at the drawn green shade.

"Pull it up; I want to see," she ordered, in a whisper.

Wearily Sue obeyed.

But, lo! after the beating rain and fierce gusts of wind that had endured through the livelong night, there yet stood out against the brick wall one ivy leaf. It was the last one on the vine. Still dark green near its stem, with its serrated edges tinted with the yellow of dissolution and decay, it hung bravely from the branch some twenty feet above the ground.

"It is the last one," said Johnsy. "I thought it would surely fall during the night. I heard the wind. It will fall to-day, and I shall die at the same time."

"Dear, dear!" said Sue, leaning her worn face down to the pillow, "think of me, if you won't think of yourself. What would I do?"

But Johnsy did not answer. The lonesomest thing in all the world is a soul when it is making ready to go on its mysterious, far journey. The fancy seemed to possess her more strongly as one by one the ties that bound her to friendship and to earth were loosed.

The day wore away, and even through the twilight they could see the lone ivy leaf clinging to its stem against the wall. And then, with the coming of the night the north wind was again loosed, while the rain still beat against the windows and pattered down from the low Dutch eaves.

When it was light enough Johnsy, the merciless, commanded that the shade be raised.

The ivy leaf was still there.

Johnsy lay for a long time looking at it. And then she called to Sue, who was stirring her chicken broth over the gas stove.

"I've been a bad girl, Sudie," said Johnsy. "Something has made that last leaf stay there to show me how wicked I was. It is a sin to want to die. You may bring a me a little broth now, and some milk with a little port in it, and--no; bring me a hand-mirror first, and then pack some pillows about me, and I will sit up and watch you cook."

And hour later she said:

"Sudie, some day I hope to paint the Bay of Naples."

The doctor came in the afternoon, and Sue had an excuse to go into the hallway as he left.

"Even chances," said the doctor, taking Sue's thin, shaking hand in his. "With good nursing you'll win." And now I must see another case I have downstairs. Behrman, his name is--some kind of an artist, I believe. Pneumonia, too. He is an old, weak man, and the attack is acute. There is no hope for him; but he goes to the hospital to-day to be made more comfortable."

The next day the doctor said to Sue: "She's out of danger. You won. Nutrition and care now--that's all."

And that afternoon Sue came to the bed where Johnsy lay, contentedly knitting a very blue and very useless woollen shoulder scarf, and put one arm around her, pillows and all.

"I have something to tell you, white mouse," she said. "Mr. Behrman died of pneumonia to-day in the hospital. He was ill only two days. The janitor found him the morning of the first day in his room downstairs helpless with pain. His shoes and clothing were wet through and icy cold. They couldn't imagine where he had been on such a dreadful night. And then they found a lantern, still lighted, and a ladder that had been dragged from its place, and some scattered brushes, and a palette with green and yellow colors mixed on it, and--look out the window, dear, at the last ivy leaf on the wall. Didn't you wonder why it never fluttered or moved when the wind blew? Ah, darling, it's Behrman's masterpiece--he painted it there the night that the last leaf fell."

12 王爾德《自私的巨人》
——淒美動人的快樂王子

奧斯卡·王爾德
（Oscar Wilde, 1854-1900）

小說特徵

悲劇性的唯美主義

We are all in the gutter, but some of us are looking at the stars.

-Oscar Wilde

我们都生活在陰溝裡，但仍有人仰望星空。

——奧斯卡·王爾德

作者短評

　　奧斯卡・王爾德（Oscar Wilde），愛爾蘭作家、詩人、戲劇家，英國唯美主義（aestheticism）倡導者。王爾德天生才氣縱橫、魅力十足，學術信念上以追求希臘美學為宗；生活上也身體力行這樣的理念，講究打扮，喜好華服的他，在當時保守的社會風氣中，雖顯得「奇裝異服、特立獨行」，王爾德卻有依然故我的自在，一如他力求維護藝術創作的本質性，成為他不變的唯美堅持。

　　王爾德有如他作品「快樂王子」，充滿著敏感與悲劇的命運特質，吸引著每一個人的目光，但同時，他特立獨行，不受世俗規範，亦招來社會眾人的側目；加上他性取向的不同，一旦勇於「出櫃」，在嚴守禮教的的英國維多利亞時代，「同志」身份注定為他帶來災難。1895年一場同性戀控告案，將王爾德如日中天的聲譽事業毀於一旦，被判入獄的同時，王爾德宣告破產，出獄後流亡法國，抑鬱而終。

　　十九世紀，王爾德和蕭伯納並列當時英國的才子，王爾德作品中所呈現悲劇性的美，為他的文創帶來極大的渲染力，足以深深地撼動人心；但真正為王爾德贏得名譽，卻是他的童話作品，王爾德寫給他的好友G. Kerstey信裡提到：「我的童話，部分是為了孩子，部分是為了那些還擁有童心的成人們。」他所寫的童話，故事結構總是呈現了淡淡的哀傷，淒美優雅，不落入俗套，卻又夾帶著幽默、戲謔的華麗文筆，抨擊社會上保守、迂腐的風氣，引起當時社會大眾的共鳴和爭議，也因為其所帶來的衝擊性，也是與一般傳統童話藝術價值不同的地方。

作品分析

　　王爾德作品與其稱之唯美主義，不如以淒美更近真實。王爾德生平除了劇作和小說之外，創作出九篇令人驚豔的童話故事，在1888年創作的《快樂王子及其他故事》（*The Happy Prince and Other Tales*）中的三篇經典故事——〈快樂王子〉裡，王子與燕子為了幫助貧苦人民，而犧牲自己；〈夜鶯與玫瑰〉中，夜鶯為了學生想要一朵紅玫瑰，結果以身體的血染紅了花瓣，綻放出美麗的紅玫瑰花朵；在〈自私的巨人〉裡，原本討厭小孩子的巨人，最終還是感受到孩童的純真，並體認到「我有許多美麗的花朵，但是孩子們才是最美的」。雖然這三則故事的結局，都存在著死亡的陰影，但感不到絲毫之可怕，反是感動，王爾德的作品，始終展現出人性中至善至美的光輝層面。

　　在王爾德的童話中，《自私的巨人》是篇幅最短的一篇，也是最富有優美、詩意的一篇。一次，王爾德給兒子講《自私的巨人》，竟然情不自禁哭了起來。兒子問他為什麼哭了，王爾德說，真正美麗的事物總會使他流下眼淚。這也是何以王爾德的故事中，往往沒有王子與公主完美結尾的戀愛故事，也沒有皆大歡喜的結局，但因為它貼近人性的一面，淒美比完美更動人，沒有happy ending的童話故事，反更有其好看之處！

The Selfish Giant

by Oscar Wilde

EVERY afternoon, as they were coming from school, the children used to go and play in the Giant's garden.

It was a large lovely garden, with soft green grass. Here and there over the grass stood beautiful flowers like stars, and there were twelve peach-trees that in the spring-time broke out into delicate blossoms of pink and pearl, and in the autumn bore rich fruit. The birds sat on the trees and sang so sweetly that the children used to stop their games in order to listen to them. "How happy we are here!" they cried to each other.

One day the Giant came back. He had been to visit his friend the Cornish ogre, and had stayed with him for seven years. After the seven years were over he had said all that he had to say, for his conversation was limited, and he determined to return to his own castle. When he arrived he saw the children playing in the garden.

"What are you doing here?" he cried in a very gruff voice, and the children ran away.

"My own garden is my own garden," said the Giant; "any one can understand that, and I will allow nobody to play in it but myself." So he built a high wall all round it, and put up a notice-board.

TRESPASSERS
WILL BE
PROSECUTED

He was a very selfish Giant.

The poor children had now nowhere to play. They tried to play on the road, but the road was very dusty and full of hard stones, and they did not like it. They used to wander round the high wall when their lessons were over, and talk about the beautiful garden inside. "How happy we were there," they said to each other.

Then the Spring came, and all over the country there were little blossoms and little birds. Only in the garden of the Selfish Giant it was still winter. The birds did not care to sing in it as there were no children, and the trees forgot to blossom. Once a beautiful flower put its head out from the grass, but when it saw the notice-board it was so sorry for the children that it slipped back into the ground again, and went off to sleep. The only people who were pleased were the Snow and the Frost. "Spring has forgotten this garden," they cried, "so we will live here all the year round." The Snow covered up the grass with her great white cloak, and the Frost painted all the trees silver. Then they invited the North Wind to stay with them, and he came. He was wrapped in furs, and he roared all day about the garden, and blew the chimney-pots down. "This is a delightful spot," he said, "we must ask the Hail on a visit." So the Hail came. Every day for three hours he rattled on the roof of the castle till he broke most of the slates, and then he ran round and round the garden as fast as he could go. He was dressed in grey, and his breath was like ice.

"I cannot understand why the Spring is so late in coming," said the Selfish Giant, as he sat at the window and looked out at his cold white garden; "I hope there will be a change in the weather."

But the Spring never came, nor the Summer. The Autumn gave golden fruit to every garden, but to the Giant's garden she gave none. "He is too selfish," she said. So it was always Winter there, and the North Wind, and the Hail, and the Frost, and the Snow danced about through the trees.

One morning the Giant was lying awake in bed when he heard some lovely music. It sounded so sweet to his ears that he thought it must be the King's musicians passing by. It was really only a little linnet singing outside his window, but it was so long since he had heard a bird sing in his garden that it seemed to him to be the most beautiful music in the world. Then the Hail stopped dancing over his head, and the North Wind ceased roaring, and a delicious perfume came to him through the open casement. "I believe the Spring has come at last," said the Giant; and he jumped out of bed and looked out.

What did he see?

He saw a most wonderful sight. Through a little hole in the wall the children had crept in, and they were sitting in the branches of the trees. In every tree that he could see there was a little child. And the trees were so glad to have the children back again that they had covered themselves with blossoms, and were waving their arms gently above the children's heads. The birds were flying about and twittering with delight, and the flowers were looking up through the green grass and laughing. It was a lovely scene, only in one corner it was still winter. It was the farthest corner of the garden, and in it was standing a little boy. He was so small that he could not reach up to the branches of the tree, and he was wandering all round it, crying bitterly. The poor tree was still quite covered with frost and snow, and the North Wind was blowing and roaring above it. "Climb up! little boy," said the Tree, and it bent its branches down as low as it could; but the boy was too tiny.

And the Giant's heart melted as he looked out. "How selfish I have been!" he said; "now I know why the Spring would not come here. I will put that poor little boy on the top of the tree, and then I will knock down the wall, and my garden shall be the children's playground for ever and ever." He was really very sorry for what he had done.

So he crept downstairs and opened the front door quite softly, and went out into the garden. But when the children saw him they were so frightened that they all ran away, and the garden became winter again. Only the little boy did not run, for his eyes were so full of tears that he did not see the Giant coming. And the Giant stole up behind him and took him gently in his hand, and put him up into the tree. And the tree broke at once into blossom, and the birds came and sang on it, and the little boy stretched out his two arms and flung them round the Giant's neck, and kissed him. And the other children, when they saw that the Giant was not wicked any longer, came running back, and with them came the Spring. "It is your garden now, little children," said the Giant, and he took a great axe and knocked down the wall. And when the people were going to market at twelve o'clock they found the Giant playing with the children in the most beautiful garden they had ever seen.

All day long they played, and in the evening they came to the Giant to bid him good-bye.

"But where is your little companion?" he said: "the boy I put into the tree." The Giant loved him the best because he had kissed him.

"We don't know," answered the children; "he has gone away."

"You must tell him to be sure and come here tomorrow," said the Giant. But the children said that they did not know where he lived, and had never seen him before; and the Giant felt very sad.

Every afternoon, when school was over, the children came and played with the Giant. But the little boy whom the Giant loved was never seen again. The Giant was very kind to all the children, yet he longed for his first little friend, and often spoke of him. "How I would like to see him!" he used to say.

Years went over, and the Giant grew very old and feeble. He could not play about any more, so he sat in a huge armchair, and watched the children at their games, and admired his garden. "I have many beautiful flowers," he said; "but the children are the most beautiful flowers of all."

One winter morning he looked out of his window as he was dressing. He did not hate the Winter now, for he knew that it was merely the Spring asleep, and that the flowers were resting.

Suddenly he rubbed his eyes in wonder, and looked and looked. It certainly was a marvellous sight. In the farthest corner of the garden was a tree quite covered with lovely white blossoms. Its branches were all golden, and silver fruit hung down from them, and underneath it stood the little boy he had loved.

Downstairs ran the Giant in great joy, and out into the garden. He hastened across the grass, and came near to the child. And when he came quite close his face grew red with anger, and he said, "Who hath dared to wound thee?" For on the palms of the child's hands were the prints of two nails, and the prints of two nails were on the little feet.

"Who hath dared to wound thee?" cried the Giant; "tell me, that I may take my big sword and slay him."

"Nay!" answered the child; "but these are the wounds of Love."

"Who art thou?" said the Giant, and a strange awe fell on him, and he knelt before the little child.

And the child smiled on the Giant, and said to him, "You let me play once in your garden, today you shall come with me to my garden, which is Paradise."

And when the children ran in that afternoon, they found the Giant lying dead under the tree, all covered with white blossoms.

13

法蘭克・史塔頓《美女還是老虎？》
──小說的創作法寶「兩難」

小說特徵

兒童文學、意外、幽默

法蘭克・史塔頓
(Frank R. Stockton, 1834-1902)

it is not for me to presume to set myself up as the one person able to answer [the question of her decision]. And so I leave it with all of you.

-Frank R. Stockton

（在故事裡），我不會把自己設定為唯一能回答問題之人，所以我把答案留給各位。

──法蘭克・史塔頓

作者短評

　　法蘭克‧史塔頓（Frank R. Stockton），1834年，出生於美國費城，由於擔任牧師的父親堅決反對史塔頓走入作家行業，史塔頓只好改以木雕維生，直到父親過世，史塔頓方才進入報社，專事於寫作，作品以幽默文風見長，但建立他文學地位則是他一系列之兒童文學作品，由於不流於同俗，廣受歡迎。

　　十九世紀下半年，美國大眾通俗文學蓬勃如雨後春筍，像是馬克‧吐溫的西部鄉土性幽默，歐亨利取材都市小人物生活故事，並以出人意外的結局取勝，同期的史塔頓則在美國文學較希罕的童話作品這一塊，兼具兩人的特色，用幽默、機智的筆觸，極力避免道德說教，在生動與幾近事實的方式下，敘述他精彩的冒險故事，挑露人性的貪心、暴力、濫權等缺憾面。他成名之作正是家喻戶曉1882年出版之《美女還是老虎？》，由於內容簡單，主題明確，史塔頓刻意保留故事結局，且反把這一任務交給了讀者，《美女還是老虎？》也成了全美甚至世界文學課堂中，最喜採用討論小說寫作的教材。

作品分析

　　小說基本就是三個要素的運作：組合「人物」（character）與「情節」（plot），用來表現「主題」（theme）的文學作品。一個有戲劇張力，能吸引讀者眼光看下去的小說，除是

「（人物）性格至（結局）命運」一以貫之的邏輯鋪陳，但精彩度仍取決情節的設計，以下有幾個小說情節設計的創作法寶－矛盾、兩難或荒謬，通常是擴大小說生動與感染讀者的有效途徑。

矛盾是內在性格與外在認定的反差，落差越大，效果越好。不論是霍桑在《紅字》中，正直虔誠的牧師卻與教友發生愛情，進而通姦生女，設計牧師掙扎於道德教義與人性慾火的矛盾之間；或國內九把刀的《殺手歐陽盆栽》也是殺手卻不殺人，反而救人，都使劇情變得有吸引力。

荒謬則是時空價值的變遷，所引起的荒謬感，譬如黃春明的《蘋果的滋味》，當窮人被美國人開車撞傷，卻是滿懷感恩與幸運的荒謬，最能勾起昨是今非的諷刺與會心一笑。

至於，兩難則是個人對外部的抉擇，效果的好壞程度，則在於抉擇的「是非」距離，如果越近－也就是當每個答案都是答案，等於沒有答案時，則越具吸引。譬如黃春明的《兒子的大玩偶》，男主角坤樹最後在工作與兒子阿龍之間，為了兒子的歡喜，只好繼續扮演自己痛恨枯燥又好笑的小丑工作。

美國幽默小說家史塔頓正是運用了這一兩難的情節，創作了一個沒有結局的故事：英俊的青年愛上了公主，卻得面對大審判，在他的面前有兩道門，一道門後面是美女；另一道門後面是老虎，他會選擇哪一道？青年望向公主，他知道她一定知道那兩扇門的祕密，他渴望公主給他暗示。公主心裡卻是掙扎萬分，她無法接受他與美女遠走高飛，重新生活，卻也不願看到愛人死亡，所以她想了很久，終於微指右邊的門，青年於是走向右邊那扇門，讀者屏息以待門打開的結果時候,故事結束了！是美女還是老虎？比歐亨利式更意外是，作者把答案的兩難留給了讀者去決定。

以筆者看法，公主介乎的兩難只是不甘的妒嫉與不捨愛人生命之間，兩難之間，道德、是非的差距太大，是個人小愛與大愛的距離，其實不難選擇，就兩難的張力言，實不如黃春明的《兒子的大玩偶》遠矣！

文選閱讀

The Lady Or The Tiger?

by Frank Stockton

In the very olden time there lived a semi-barbaric king, whose ideas, though somewhat polished and sharpened by the progressiveness of distant Latin neighbors, were still large, florid, and untrammeled, as became the half of him which was barbaric.

When a subject was accused of a crime of sufficient importance to interest the king, public notice was given that on an appointed day the fate of the accused person would be decided in the king's arena, a structure which well deserved its name, for, although its form and plan were borrowed from afar, its purpose emanated solely from the brain of this man, who, every barleycorn a king, knew no tradition to which he owed more allegiance than pleased his fancy, and who ingrafted on every adopted form of human thought and action the rich growth of his barbaric idealism.

When all the people had assembled in the galleries, and the king, surrounded by his court, sat high up on his throne of royal state on one side of the arena, he gave a signal, a door beneath him opened, and the accused subject stepped out into the amphitheater. Directly opposite him, on the other side of the enclosed space, were two doors, exactly alike and side by side. It was the duty and the privilege of the person on trial to walk directly to these doors and open one of them. He could open either door he pleased; he was subject to no guidance or influence but that of the aforementioned impartial and incorruptible chance. If he opened the one, there came out of it a hungry tiger, the fiercest and most cruel that could be procured, which immediately sprang upon him and tore him to pieces as a punishment for his guilt.

But, if the accused person opened the other door, there came forth from it a lady, the most suitable to his years and station that his majesty could select among his fair subjects, and to this lady he was immediately married, as a reward of his innocence. It mattered not that he might already possess a wife and family, or that his affections might be engaged upon an object of his own selection; the king allowed no such subordinate arrangements to interfere with his great scheme of retribution and reward.

This was the king's semi-barbaric method of administering justice. Its perfect fairness is obvious. The criminal could not know out of which door would come the lady; he opened either he pleased, without having the slightest idea whether, in the next instant, he was to be devoured or married. On some occasions the tiger came out of one door, and on some out of the other. The decisions of this tribunal were not only fair, they were positively determinate: the accused person was instantly punished if he found himself guilty, and, if innocent, he was rewarded on the spot, whether he liked it or not. There was no escape from the judgments of the king's arena.

The institution was a very popular one. When the people gathered together on one of the great trial days, they never knew whether they were to witness a bloody slaughter or a hilarious wedding. This element of uncertainty lent an interest to the occasion which it could not otherwise have attained. Thus, the masses were entertained and pleased, and the thinking part of the community could bring no charge of unfairness against this plan, for did not the accused person have the whole matter in his own hands?

This semi-barbaric king had a daughter as blooming as his most florid fancies, and with a soul as fervent and imperious as his own. As is usual in such cases, she was the apple of his eye, and was loved by him above all humanity. Among his courtiers was a young man of that fineness of blood and lowness of station common to the conventional heroes of romance who love royal maidens. This royal maiden was well satisfied with her lover, for he was handsome and brave to a degree unsurpassed in all this kingdom, and she loved him with an ardor that had enough of barbarism in it to make it exceedingly warm and strong. This love affair moved on happily for many months, until one day the king happened to discover its existence. He did not hesitate nor waver in regard to his duty in the premises. The youth was immediately cast into prison, and a day was appointed for his trial in the king's arena. This, of course, was an especially important occasion, and his majesty, as well as all the people, was greatly interested in the workings and development of this trial. Never before had such a case occurred; never before had a subject dared to love the daughter of the king. In after years such things became commonplace enough, but then they were in no slight degree novel and startling.

The tiger-cages of the kingdom were searched for the most savage and relentless beasts, from which the fiercest monster might be selected for the arena; and the ranks of maiden youth and beauty throughout the land were carefully surveyed by competent judges in order that the young man might have a fitting bride in case fate did not determine for him a different destiny. Of course, everybody knew that the deed with which the accused was charged had been done. He had loved the princess, and neither he, she, nor any one else, thought of denying the fact; but the king would not think of allowing any fact of this kind to interfere with the workings of the tribunal, in which he took such great delight and satisfaction. No matter how the affair turned out, the youth would be disposed of, and the king would take an aesthetic pleasure in watching the course of events, which would determine whether or not the young man had done wrong in allowing himself to love the princess.

The appointed day arrived. From far and near the people gathered, and thronged the great galleries of the arena, and crowds, unable to gain admittance, massed themselves against its outside walls. The king and his court were in their places, opposite the twin doors, those fateful portals, so terrible in their similarity.

All was ready. The signal was given. A door beneath the royal party opened, and the lover of the princess walked into the arena. Tall, beautiful, fair, his appearance was greeted with a low hum of admiration and anxiety. Half the audience had not known so grand a youth had lived among them. No wonder the princess loved him! What a terrible thing for him to be there!

As the youth advanced into the arena he turned, as the custom was, to bow to the king, but he did not think at all of that royal personage. His eyes were fixed upon the princess, who sat to the right of her father. Had it not been for the moiety of barbarism in her nature it is probable that lady would not have been there, but her intense and fervid soul would not allow her to be absent on an occasion in which she was so terribly interested.

From the moment that the decree had gone forth that her lover should decide his fate in the king's arena, she had thought of nothing, night or day, but this great event and the various subjects connected with it. Possessed of more power, influence, and force of character than any one who had ever before been interested in such a case, she had done what no other person had done – she had possessed herself of the secret of the doors. She knew in which of the two rooms, that lay behind those doors, stood the cage of the tiger, with its open front, and in which waited the lady. Through these thick doors, heavily curtained with skins on the inside, it was impossible that any noise or suggestion should come from within to the person who should approach to raise the latch of one of them. But gold, and the power of a woman's will, had brought the secret to the princess.

And not only did she know in which room stood the lady ready to emerge, all blushing and radiant, should her door be opened, but she knew who the lady was. It was one of the fairest and loveliest of the damsels of the court who had been selected as the reward of the accused youth, should he be proved innocent of the crime of aspiring to one so far above him; and the princess hated her. Often had she seen, or imagined that she had seen, this fair creature throwing glances of admiration upon the person of her lover, and sometimes she thought these glances were perceived, and even returned. Now and then she had seen them talking together; it was but for a moment or two, but much can be said in a brief space; it may have been on most unimportant topics, but how could she know that? The girl was lovely, but she had dared to raise her eyes to the loved one of the princess; and, with all the intensity of the savage blood transmitted to her through long lines of wholly barbaric ancestors, she hated the woman who blushed and trembled behind that silent door.

When her lover turned and looked at her, and his eye met hers as she sat there, paler and whiter than any one in the vast ocean of anxious faces about her, he saw, by that power of quick perception which is given to those whose souls are one, that she knew behind which door crouched the tiger, and behind which stood the lady. He had expected her to know it. He understood her nature, and his soul was assured that she would never rest until she had made plain to herself this thing, hidden to all other lookers-on, even to the king. The only hope for the youth in which there was any element of certainty was based upon the success of the princess in discovering this mystery; and the moment he looked upon her, he saw she had succeeded, as in his soul he knew she would succeed.

Then it was that his quick and anxious glance asked the question: "Which?" It was as plain to her as if he shouted it from where he stood. There was not an instant to be lost. The question was asked in a flash; it must be answered in another.

Her right arm lay on the cushioned parapet before her. She raised her hand, and made a slight, quick movement toward the right. No one but her lover saw her. Every eye but his was fixed on the man in the arena.

He turned, and with a firm and rapid step he walked across the empty space. Every heart stopped beating, every breath was held, every eye was fixed immovably upon that man. Without the slightest hesitation, he went to the door on the right, and opened it.

Now, the point of the story is this: Did the tiger come out of that door, or did the lady ?

The more we reflect upon this question, the harder it is to answer. It involves a study of the human heart which leads us through devious mazes of passion, out of which it is difficult to find our way. Think of it, fair reader, not as if the decision of the question depended upon yourself, but upon that hot-blooded, semi-barbaric princess, her soul at a white heat beneath the combined fires of despair and jealousy. She had lost him, but who should have him?

How often, in her waking hours and in her dreams, had she started in wild horror, and covered her face with her hands as she thought of her lover opening the door on the other side of which waited the cruel fangs of the tiger!

But how much oftener had she seen him at the other door! How in her grievous reveries had she gnashed her teeth, and torn her hair, when she saw his start of rapturous delight as he opened the door of the lady! How her soul had burned in agony when she had seen him rush to meet that woman, with her flushing cheek and sparkling eye of triumph; when she had seen him lead her forth, his whole frame kindled with the joy of recovered life; when she had heard the glad shouts from the multitude, and the wild ringing of the happy bells; when she had seen the priest, with his joyous followers, advance to the couple, and make them man and wife before her very eyes; and when she had seen them walk away together upon their path of flowers, followed by the tremendous shouts of the hilarious multitude, in which her one despairing shriek was lost and drowned!

Would it not be better for him to die at once, and go to wait for her in the blessed regions of semi-barbaric futurity?

And yet, that awful tiger, those shrieks, that blood!

Her decision had been indicated in an instant, but it had been made after days and nights of anguished deliberation. She had known she would be asked, she had decided what she would answer, and, without the slightest hesitation, she had moved her hand to the right.

The question of her decision is one not to be lightly considered, and it is not for me to presume to set myself up as the one person able to answer it. And so I leave it with all of you: Which came out of the opened door – the lady, or the tiger ?

喬伊斯《伊芙琳》
——小說之蒙太奇大師

詹姆斯‧喬伊斯
（James Joyce, 1882-1941）

小說特徵

愛爾蘭鄉土情懷，意識流
（Stream of Consciousness）

All the seas of the world tumbled about her heart. He was drawing her into them: he would drown her. She gripped with both hands at the iron railing.

-James Joyce, Eveline

世界所有的海水湧入她的內心。他正拉她入海，使她淹沒。她雙手緊抓鐵欄杆不放。

——喬伊斯，《伊芙琳》

作者短評

　　詹姆斯·喬伊斯（James Joyce），1882年，出生於愛爾蘭都柏林的一富裕天主教家庭，但喬伊斯父親的酗酒以及對財產的管理不善，家庭旋由富裕變貧窮，在喬伊斯的小說中，反覆出現的父親角色，正是他以自己父親形象之塑造。

　　喬伊斯大學畢業後到巴黎、蘇黎世等地過著流浪生活，1920年至1939年期間定居法國。儘管喬伊斯一生大部分時光都遠離故土愛爾蘭，但極重鄉土意識的他，他小說中故事的發生大多根植於他早年在都柏林的生活，包括他的家庭、朋友、敵人、中學和大學的歲月，喬伊斯早期出版的短篇小說集《都柏林人》（1914）就是深入剖析都柏林社會發展的遲緩和麻木，也從這部小說中，喬伊斯深刻的故土懷情，藉由意識流技巧的發揮，初露端倪，他運用大量心理獨白，而且更多的關注於人的內心世界而非客觀現實的表達。

　　喬伊斯最大成就是在全面推進和發展意識流小說，帶領此一文學流派邁上顛峰。意識流文學是對尋常人物內心世界的複雜活動，提供更真實的描述，包括清醒的意識，更包括無意識、夢幻意識和語言前意識，天馬行空，想像不受時空拘束的技巧。喬伊斯於1906年完成《都柏林人》之後，便開始構思新的小說《尤利西斯》，大量採用了意識流技巧，故事發生地點是都柏林，將古希臘神話融入現代文學的敘事結構，這部小說的全部故事情節都發生在一天之內：1904年6月16日。《尤利西斯》全書分為十八個章節，每個章節講述一天中一個小時之內發生的事，是意識流文學的極緻之作，樹立喬依思小說大師地位。

作品分析

現代主義小說中，意識流是一個特殊的學派。意識流小說家對傳統小說中，作者主導人物身世與內在、外界環境，間或挺身而出，對角色評頭論足，認為毫無必要；時空排列上，也不循傳統小說時間與空間的編年直線前進，可說是小說寫創上極大之革命，喬伊斯主張消滅作者人格的戲劇，認為沒有作者意識的作品是最高的美學形式，並力圖在小說中達到這一目標。

「意識流」最初見於美國心理學家威廉・詹姆斯，他認為人類的意識活動是一種連續不斷的流動狀態。二十世紀初，佛洛伊德的下意識和夢與藝術關係的理論，都對意識流文學的發展有重大影響。由於其技巧獨特，意識流文學在概念與技巧上的特徵有（一）內心獨白：純粹是小說中人物自己的真實意識流露。個人把所感所思，毫無顧忌的直接表露出來。（二）內心分析：個人對自己非意識自然流動的思想和感受進行分析探索。（三）自由聯想：人物的意識流表現，不受任何規律和次序限制，眼前任何能刺激五官的事物，都能打斷人物的思路，激發新的思緒與浮想，釋放一連串的印象和感觸。（四）時間和空間蒙太奇：意識流小說家突破時空的限制，表現意識流動的多變性、複雜性。

本文所挑選之《伊芙琳》（Eveline），是喬伊斯的短篇小說集《都柏林人》中的一篇，描繪都柏林人們的生存狀態，表現這座城市的貧窮和枯燥。這部小說對都柏林的描繪可謂細緻入微，敘述一位女子伊芙琳不甘浪費生命，繼續蟄伏在沒落故鄉，決心與愛人法蘭克私奔，卻又不捨故人鄉土的內心掙扎，相較上，意識流的小說技巧自比傳統方法，更能探微人心細膩之活動。全文描寫十九歲少女伊芙琳在與法蘭克私奔前，最後對故鄉愛爾蘭與家之眷念，初從家中窗簾布，想著為何有這麼多打掃不完的灰塵、幼時遊玩如今卻蓋上房子的大庭院、父親的兇悍、家務的操勞、商店同事的尖酸刻薄與母親一生的作牛作馬；但心情一轉，又對窗簾布氣味的眷戀，想到她在母親死前，答應照顧家庭的承諾，父親也有溫暖貼心的時刻，內心轉生猶豫不捨的心情，最後，在上船前的一刻，愛情與家人的拉扯心情像是驚濤駭浪，當下，她決定放棄離開這個家，對法蘭克有如大海襲來般的催促，伊芙琳只有回望法蘭克，「她的眼神沒有一絲愛戀或即將離別的跡象，也沒有曾經熟稔的表情。」，讓抽象的意識有了體溫、氣味與視覺，動人心弦。

Eveline

by James Joyce

SHE sat at the window watching the evening invade the avenue. Her head was leaned against the window curtains and in her nostrils was the odour of dusty cretonne. She was tired.

Few people passed. The man out of the last house passed on his way home; she heard his footsteps clacking along the concrete pavement and afterwards crunching on the cinder path before the new red houses. One time there used to be a field there in which they used to play every evening with other people's children. Then a man from Belfast bought the field and built houses in it--not like their little brown houses but bright brick houses with shining roofs. The children of the avenue used to play together in that field--the Devines, the Waters, the Dunns, little Keogh the cripple, she and her brothers and sisters. Ernest, however, never played: he was too grown up. Her father used often to hunt them in out of the field with his blackthorn stick; but usually little Keogh used to keep nix and call out when he saw her father coming. Still they seemed to have been rather happy then. Her father was not so bad then; and besides, her mother was alive. That was a long time ago; she and her brothers and sisters were all grown up her mother was dead. Tizzie Dunn was dead, too, and the Waters had gone back to England. Everything changes. Now she was going to go away like the others, to leave her home.

Home! She looked round the room, reviewing all its familiar objects which she had dusted once a week for so many years, wondering where on earth all the dust came from. Perhaps she would never see again those familiar objects from which she had never dreamed of being divided. And yet during all those years she had never found out the name of the priest whose yellowing photograph hung on the wall above the broken harmonium beside the coloured print of the promises made to Blessed Margaret Mary Alacoque. He had been a school friend of her father. Whenever he showed the photograph to a visitor her father used to pass it with a casual word:

"He is in Melbourne now."

She had consented to go away, to leave her home. Was that wise? She tried to weigh each side of the question. In her home anyway she had shelter and food; she had those whom she had known all her life about her. O course she had to work hard, both in the house and at business. What would they say of her in the Stores when they found out that she had run away with a fellow? Say she was a fool, perhaps; and her place would be filled up by advertisement. Miss Gavan would be glad. She had always had an edge on her, especially whenever there were people listening.

"Miss Hill, don't you see these ladies are waiting?"

"Look lively, Miss Hill, please."

She would not cry many tears at leaving the Stores.

But in her new home, in a distant unknown country, it would not be like that. Then she would be married--she, Eveline. People would treat her with respect then. She would not be treated as her mother had been. Even now, though she was over nineteen, she sometimes felt herself in danger of her father's violence. She knew it was that that had given her the palpitations. When they were growing up he had never gone for her like he used to go for Harry and Ernest, because she was a girl but latterly he had begun to threaten her and say what he would do to her only for her dead mother's sake. And no she had nobody to protect her. Ernest was dead and Harry, who was in the church decorating business, was nearly always down somewhere in the country. Besides, the invariable squabble for money on Saturday nights had begun to weary her unspeakably. She always gave her entire wages--seven shillings--and Harry always sent up what he could but the trouble was to get any money from her father. He said she used to squander the money, that she had no head, that he wasn't going to give her his hard-earned money to throw about the streets, and much more, for he was usually fairly bad on Saturday night. In the end he would give her the money and ask her had she any intention of buying Sunday's dinner. Then she had to rush out as quickly as she could and do her marketing, holding her black leather purse tightly in her hand as she elbowed her way through the crowds and returning home late under her load of provisions. She had hard work to keep the house together and to see that the two young children who had been left to hr charge went to school regularly and got their meals regularly. It was hard work--a hard life--but now that she was about to leave it she did not find it a wholly undesirable life.

She was about to explore another life with Frank. Frank was very kind, manly, open-hearted. She was to go away with him by the night-boat to be his wife and to live with him in Buenos Ayres where he had a home waiting for her. How well she remembered the first time she had seen him; he was lodging in a house on the main road where she used to visit. It seemed a few weeks ago. He was standing at the gate, his peaked cap pushed back on his head and his hair tumbled forward over a face of bronze. Then they had come to know each other. He used to meet her outside the Stores every evening and see her home. He took her to see The Bohemian Girl and she felt elated as she sat in an unaccustomed part of the theatre with him. He was awfully fond of music and sang a little. People knew that they were courting and, when he sang about the lass that loves a sailor, she always felt pleasantly confused. He used to call her Poppens out of fun. First of all it had been an excitement for her to have a fellow and then she had begun to like him. He had tales of distant countries. He had started as a deck boy at a pound a month on a ship of the Allan Line going out to Canada. He told her the names of the ships he had been on and the names of the different services. He had sailed through the Straits of Magellan and he told her stories of the terrible Patagonians. He had fallen on his feet in Buenos Ayres, he said, and had come over to the old country just for a holiday. Of course, her father had found out the affair and had forbidden her to have anything to say to him.

"I know these sailor chaps," he said.

One day he had quarrelled with Frank and after that she had to meet her lover secretly.

The evening deepened in the avenue. The white of two letters in her lap grew indistinct. One was to Harry; the other was to her father. Ernest had been her favourite but she liked Harry too. Her father was becoming old lately, she noticed; he would miss her. Sometimes he could be very nice. Not long before, when she had been laid up for a day, he had read her out a ghost story and made toast for her at the fire. Another day, when their mother was alive, they had all gone for a picnic to the Hill of Howth. She remembered her father putting on her mothers bonnet to make the children laugh.

Her time was running out but she continued to sit by the window, leaning her head against the window curtain, inhaling the odour of dusty cretonne. Down far in the avenue she could hear a street organ playing. She knew the air Strange that it should come that very night to remind her of the promise to her mother, her promise to keep the home together as long as she could. She remembered the last night of her mother's illness; she was again in the close dark room at the other side of the hall and outside she heard a melancholy air of Italy. The organ-player had been ordered to go away and given sixpence. She remembered her father strutting back into the sickroom saying:

"Damned Italians! coming over here!"

As she mused the pitiful vision of her mother's life laid its spell on the very quick of her being--that life of commonplace sacrifices closing in final craziness. She trembled as she heard again her mother's voice saying constantly with foolish insistence:

"Derevaun Seraun! Derevaun Seraun!"

She stood up in a sudden impulse of terror. Escape! She must escape! Frank would save her. He would give her life, perhaps love, too. But she wanted to live. Why should she be unhappy? She had a right to happiness. Frank would take her in his arms, fold her in his arms. He would save her.

She stood among the swaying crowd in the station at the North Wall. He held her hand and she knew that he was speaking to her, saying something about the passage over and over again. The station was full of soldiers with brown baggages. Through the wide doors of the sheds she caught a glimpse of the black mass of the boat, lying in beside the quay wall, with illumined portholes. She answered nothing. She felt her cheek pale and cold and, out of a maze of distress, she prayed to God to direct her, to show her what was her duty. The boat blew a long mournful whistle into the mist. If she went, tomorrow she would be on the sea with Frank, steaming towards Buenos Ayres. Their passage had been booked. Could she still draw back after all he had done for her? Her distress awoke a nausea in her body and she kept moving her lips in silent fervent prayer.

A bell clanged upon her heart. She felt him seize her hand:

"Come!"

All the seas of the world tumbled about her heart. He was drawing her into them: he would drown her. She gripped with both hands at the iron railing.

"Come!"

No! No! No! It was impossible. Her hands clutched the iron in frenzy. Amid the seas she sent a cry of anguish.

"Eveline! Evvy!"

He rushed beyond the barrier and called to her to follow. He was shouted at to go on but he still called to her. She set her white face to him, passive, like a helpless animal. Her eyes gave him no sign of love or farewell or recognition.

伍爾芙《一間鬼屋》
——內心更潛深處之探索

弗吉尼亞·伍爾芙
(Virginia Woolf, 1882-1941)

小說特徵

性別、女權與意識流

*A woman must have money and a room of her own if she is to write
fiction.*

-Virginia Woolf

女性若是想要寫作，一定要有錢和自己的房間（空間）。
——弗吉尼亞·伍爾芙

作者短評

　　小說作家之異於常人者，不外敏銳過人，多愁善感，以致常「衣帶漸寬終不悔，為伊消得人憔悴」，伍爾芙即此極端之例。在失去正常女人親情、愛情以至婚姻、家庭的代價下，伍爾芙一生活在憂鬱症的精神煉獄中，承受著如火山熔岩的折磨，煅煉出如晶如鑽之作品，大放人世光芒。

　　弗吉尼亞・伍爾芙（Virginia Woolf），1882年，生於倫敦，她和詹姆斯・喬伊斯（巧合是兩人也是生死同年）都是運用意識流的寫作方法，去描繪沉底人心的潛意識，極大地影響了傳統的小說寫作手法，為傳統文學和現代文學劃下分水嶺，公認是二十世紀意識流作家中成就最高的女性，也是現代主義與女性主義先鋒。

　　伍爾芙出身書香門第，家世顯赫，自幼精神脆弱，卻天性敏感，具有不可思議的理解力和敏銳觀察的邏輯，她幾乎可以看到別人的內心深處，寫出那些別人無法表達出來的奧秘思緒，這也許是她會成為意識流小說大家的原因，但無疑也是伴隨了她一生的痼疾：憂鬱症的根源，伍爾芙一生就在精神崩潰，憂鬱痛楚的狀態下，寫出不朽作品。

　　伍爾芙對於別人有關她作品的評價極為敏感，甚至到了神經質的狀態，由於她的精神分裂症狀越來越嚴重，她在自傳《存在的瞬間》（*Moments of Being*）中透露了小時候受到家庭性侵，讓她的身心受到極大摧殘，心中留下陰影，以致她一生厭惡性行為，不願生育，不和丈夫同房。1941年3月28日，伍爾芙毫無留戀，一步一步向河中心走去，慢慢地沉入了水的深處，結束了自己短暫的一生。艾略特（T.S. Eliot）認為伍爾芙是當時英國文學的中心，是一種文明模式的代表。她的逝世意味着一個時代的結束。

作品分析

　　傳統小說若像一幅寫實畫，伍爾芙的小說觀點就像後印象主義畫派的抽象安排。伍爾芙與其他男性意識流作家不同之處在於，她的小說往往富有詩意，在語言上更像詩體散文，富有唯美主義的情調，描寫單位由社群轉至個人，由外部感官導入內部知覺，由生理移向心理，其敘事觀點也由第三人稱的全知轉成全面的心理獨白，時空自由穿梭，發展出一個獨立的虛構世界；其內在獨白之深邃，所傳達出個人內心複雜的感受，是意識流的高峰之作，但其小說內容的晦澀難懂卻和其他意識流作家的作品別無二致。

　　在其代表作《一間鬼屋》中，描述一對百年前死亡，重回舊巢的男女鬼魂，作者沒有設計貫串全文的解說情節，而是時刻強調「瞬間」感覺的重要性，認為生命的本質在於感覺。伍爾芙高明的安排在一間屋內，卻是陰、陽兩界，一生一死的兩對夫婦男女，彼此的相互觀察與互動，主題則是尋找屋中的寶藏。伍爾芙為意識流更創新境，以屋中的一面的玻璃窗戶，隔開了陰、陽兩界的動線，像不像印象畫派光影視覺的文字享

受，讓這間房子有了栩栩如生的心跳，直到這對鬼魂夫婦凝視
屋中夫婦安詳的沉睡狀態，才找到了屋中的寶藏，就是昔日兩
人共處歡樂無憂的美好時光！

文選閱讀

A Haunted House

by Virginia Woolf

WHATEVER hour you woke there was a door shunting. From room to room they went, hand in hand, lifting here, opening there, making sure--a ghostly couple.

"Here we left it," she said. And he added, "Oh, but here too!" "It's upstairs," she murmured. "And in the garden," he whispered "Quietly," they said, "or we shall wake them."

But it wasn't that you woke us. "Oh, no." They're looking for it; they're drawing the curtain, one might say, and so read on a page or two. "Now they've found it," one would be certain, stopping the pencil on the margin. And then, tired of reading, one might rise and see for oneself, the house all empty, the doors standing open, only the wood pigeons bubbling with content and the hum of the threshing machine sounding from the farm. "What did I come in here for? What did I want to find?" My hands were empty. "Perhaps it's upstairs then?" The apples were in the loft. And so down again, the garden still as ever, only the book had slipped into the grass.

But they had found it in the drawing room. Not that one could ever see them. The window panes reflected apples, reflected roses; all the leaves were green in the glass. If they moved in the drawing room, the apple only turned its yellow side. Yet, the moment after, if the door was opened, spread about the floor, hung upon the walls, pendant from the ceiling-- what? My hands were empty. The shadow of a thrush crossed the carpet; from the deepest wells of silence the wood pigeon drew its bubble of sound. "Safe, safe, safe," the pulse of the house beat softly. "The treasure buried; the room..." the pulse stopped short. Oh, was that the buried treasure?

A moment later the light had faded. Out in the garden then? But the trees spun darkness for a wandering beam of sun. So fine, so rare, coolly sunk beneath the surface the beam I sought always burnt behind the glass. Death was the glass; death was between us; coming to the woman first, hundreds of years ago, leaving the house, sealing all the windows; the rooms were darkened. He left it, left her, went North, went East, saw the stars turned in the Southern sky; sought the house, found it dropped beneath the Downs. "Safe, safe, safe," the pulse of the house beat gladly. "The Treasure yours."

The wind roars up the avenue. Trees stoop and bend this way and that. Moonbeams splash and spill wildly in the rain. But the beam of the lamp falls straight from the window. The candle burns stiff and still. Wandering through the house, opening the windows, whispering not to wake us, the ghostly couple seek their joy.

"Here we slept," she says. And he adds, "Kisses without number." "Waking in the morning;" "Silver between the trees;" "Upstairs;" "In the garden;" "When summer came;" "In winter snowtime;" The doors go shutting far in the distance, gently knocking like the pulse of a heart.

Nearer they come; cease at the doorway. The wind falls, the rain slides silver down the glass. Our eyes darken; we hear no steps beside us; we see no lady spread her ghostly cloak. His hands shield the lantern. "Look," he breathes. "Sound asleep. Love upon their lips."

Stooping, holding their silver lamp above us, long they look and deeply. Long they pause. The wind drives straightly; the flame stoops slightly. Wild beams of moonlight cross both floor and wall, and, meeting, stain the faces bent; the faces pondering; the faces that search the sleepers and seek their hidden joy.

"Safe, safe, safe," the heart of the house beats proudly. "Long years;" he sighs. "Again you found me." "Here," she murmurs, "sleeping; in the garden reading; laughing, rolling apples in the loft. Here we left our treasure;" Stooping, their light lifts the lids upon my eyes. "Safe! safe! safe!" the pulse of the house beats wildly. Waking, I cry "Oh, is this *your* buried treasure? The light in the heart."

16 馬克‧吐溫《好小孩的故事》
——美國西部幽默文學之父

小說特徵

美國西部風土、人情的口語
化幽默

馬克‧吐溫
(Mark Twain, 1835-1910)

Humor is the great thing, the saving thing. The minute it crops up, all our irritations and resentments slip away and a sunny spirit takes their place.

-Mark Twain

幽默是最棒的事,是救人的東西。當幽默一來,我們所有的不悅與憤怒都會走開,一個充滿陽光的精神會取而代之。

——馬克‧吐溫

　　馬克‧吐溫，原名山姆‧克萊門斯（Samuel Langhorne Clemens），1835年，出生於美國密蘇里州的小城佛羅里達（Florida），在他四歲的時候，全家遷往緊鄰密西西比河畔的小鎮漢尼拔（Hannibal），他日後小說《湯姆歷險記》（*The Adventures of Tom Sawyer*）和《哈克芬恩歷險記》（*Adventures of Huckleberry Finn*）的素材，即來自這個密西西比河港小鎮的風土人情。

　　所謂「靠山吃山，靠水吃水」，馬克‧吐溫生來與密西西比河為伍，對這條縱橫南北，隔開東岸「文明」，象徵大西部的大河，情感濃厚。馬克‧吐溫自小立志當個汽船領航員，「馬克‧吐溫」靈感即來自密西西比河上測水人的術語，意指「水深兩潯」（two fathoms：約3.7米）的意思。二十三歲時，他終於取得了正式領航員的資格，但沒多久，南北戰爭開始，密西西比河的航行中斷，馬克‧吐溫失去了領航員的職務。由於密蘇里州恰處美國南北界標的模糊地帶，居民應屬南軍或北軍，莫衷一是，馬克‧吐溫後來雖被劃歸南軍，但只當了兩星期的南軍便「落跑」，旋即到西部淘金，歷盡大平原、洛磯山脈、甚至摩門教之鹽湖城，一年後，無功而返，轉行進入新聞報業，而這些美國大西部之所見所聞，正好提供了他日後踏入文壇的寫作能量。馬克‧吐溫犀利、口語化的幽默文筆，大受人民歡迎，瞬間，取得全國性的名氣，樹立馬克‧吐溫的文豪地位。馬克・吐溫於1865年10月，在給他弟弟信中談到了他決心接受「上帝的召喚」，去從事「上帝要他作的事」，換言之，即是寫幽默文學，透過笑聲來鼓舞人類精神，這些感覺在他作品的字裡行間，格外深刻且生動。

馬克・吐溫出生時，恰逢哈雷彗星劃越地球，彷彿是來自天上的賀禮，馬克・吐溫因此一直以為他也會乘哈雷彗星而去，1910年4月21日，馬克・吐溫在美國康乃狄格州因心臟病去世，一天後，哈雷彗星果然再度光臨，劃空而去，彷彿接走在人間75年的馬克・吐溫，重歸天際。

作品分析

國與國間因地理知不同而有文化差異，其實，一國之內也不免地域之有別，而生人民之不同。美國地域的差異，我們一般將注意力放在南北方向，像是兩地對黑人民權、經濟發展或自由保守看法，由於相較極端，自易引人矚目。但在南北問題之餘，美國也有東西的文化差別，只是他們不同南北問題那樣的火爆與激烈。馬克・吐溫正是深刻注意到東、西部文化不同的作家，他對美國大西部純樸、直接的泥土味，一直認為是保有美國獨立精神的理想夢奇地，而西部的美國人——豪邁、粗獷、不拘禮節的個性，更被馬克・吐溫認定是忠於原味的美國人，深深有別於東部在文明禮俗調教（tamed）後的美國人。

馬克・吐溫1865年的成名之作《坎拉貝斯城有名的跳蛙》，即著筆東部文明與西部拓荒地兩者之間的價值衝突，暗喻對東部人的道德諷刺，敘述一位來自西部，樂觀、心地單純的賭徒史邁利，在一場「跳蛙」比賽中，敗給了使詐的東部人，不論是形容賽馬、鬥狗與跳蛙的動作，如「青蛙在空中躍騰如同旋轉的甜圈圈、落地如貓」，以及東部人使詐將鉛彈灌進跳蛙嘴巴的技倆，比賽時，跳蛙挺了一下「聳起肩膀－活像個法國人，毫無用處──像教堂一樣穩固，膠著在那裡」，這種對獨特細節之具體用心及化諸口語式幽默文學，生動純真，維妙維肖，引人發噱，這也是馬克・吐溫總是以幽默的態度敘事，而不是嚴厲地去批判文化上的對立，以致他故事的成功主因。

　　本書所選同時寫於1865年的《好小孩的故事》，馬克・吐溫以更坦白、嘲諷、誇張幽默的筆調，敘述一位孩童Jacob Blivens，他循規蹈矩，行為品性好到離譜，卻顯得老氣橫秋、食古不化，所有同齡小孩平常打彈子、抓鳥到調皮、惡作劇的事一概不作，力行主日學的教條，不但要作最乖的小孩，還要教導壞小孩（bad boys）改邪歸正，結果Jacob Blivens的遭遇根本不是這回事，他要壞小孩不要爬樹偷摘蘋果，壞小孩跌下來卻是壓傷他；他制止壞小孩偷玩帆船，結果自己跌下水，他用滿紙老師稱讚的介紹信應徵船員，被船長奚落不切實際，最後好小孩在制止壞小孩欺負狗時被炸得粉身碎骨，「穿過屋頂，飛向太陽，後連著十五條狗的身體殘餘，就像風箏後面的尾穗一般」，全文充滿美國西部人豪放、不在乎的語調，暗諷現代文明與宗教的教條，讓小孩失去了最可愛的童稚與赤子之心，不斷讓讀者腦海浮現出《湯姆歷險記》中，那位靈活、頑皮，一身是膽的西部小孩，才是馬克・吐溫渴望的美國典型。

文選閱讀

The Story of the Good Little Boy

by Mark Twain

Once there was a good little boy by the name of Jacob Blivens. He always obeyed his parents, no matter how absurd and unreasonable their demands were; and he always learned his book, and never was late at Sabbath-school. He would not play hookey, even when his sober judgment told him it was the most profitable thing he could do. None of the other boys could ever make that boy out, he acted so strangely. He couldn't lie, no matter how convenient it was. He just said it was wrong to lie, and that was sufficient for him. And he was so honest that he was simply ridiculous. The curious ways that Jacob had, surpassed everything. He wouldn't play marbles on Sunday, he wouldn't rob birds' nests, he wouldn't give hot pennies to organ-grinders' monkeys; he didn't seem to take any interest in any kind of rational amusement. So the other boys used to try to reason it out and come to an understanding of him, but they couldn't arrive at any satisfactory conclusion. As I said before, they could only figure out a sort of vague idea that he was "afflicted," and so they took him under their protection, and never allowed any harm to come to him.

This good little boy read all the Sunday-school books; they were his greatest delight. This was the whole secret of it. He believed in the good little boys they put in the Sunday-school books; he had every confidence in them. He longed to come across one of them alive once; but he never did. They all died before his time, maybe. Whenever he read about a particularly good one he turned over quickly to the end to see what became of him, but it wasn't any use; that good little boy always died in the last chapter, and there was a picture of the funeral, with all his relations and the Sunday-school children standing around the grave and everybody crying into handkerchiefs...

Jacob had a noble ambition to be put in a Sunday-school book. He wanted to be put in, with pictures representing him gloriously declining to lie to his mother, and her weeping for joy about it; and pictures representing him standing on the doorstep giving a penny to a poor beggar-woman with six children, and telling her to spend it freely, but not to be extravagant, because extravagance is a sin; and pictures of him magnanimously refusing to tell on the bad boy who always lay in wait for him around the corner as he came from school, and welted him over the head with a lath, and then chased him home, saying, "Hi! hi!" as he proceeded. That was the ambition of young Jacob Blivens. He wished to be put in a Sunday-school book. It made him feel a little uncomfortable sometimes when he reflected that the good little boys always died. He loved to live, you know, and this was the most unpleasant feature about being a Sunday-school-book boy... it pained him to think that if they put him in a book he wouldn't ever see it, or even if they did get the book out before he died it wouldn't be popular without any picture of his funeral in the back part of it. It couldn't be much of a Sunday-school book that couldn't tell about the advice he gave to the community when he was dying. So at last, of course, he had to make up his mind to do the best he could under the circumstances to live right, and hang on as long as he could, and have his dying speech all ready when his time came.

But somehow nothing ever went right with this good little boy;

nothing ever turned out with him the way it turned out with the good little boys in the books. They always had a good time, and the bad boys had the broken legs; but in his case there was a screw loose somewhere, and it all happened just the other way. When he found Jim Blake stealing apples, and went under the tree to read to him about the bad little boy who fell out of a neighbor's apple tree and broke his arm, Jim fell out of the tree, too, but he fell on him and broke his arm, and Jim wasn't hurt at all. Jacob couldn't understand that. There wasn't anything in the books like it.

And once, when some bad boys pushed a blind man over in the mud, and Jacob ran to help him up and receive his blessing, the blind man did not give him any blessing at all, but whacked him over the head with his stick and said he would like to catch him shoving him again, and then pretending to help him up. This was not in accordance with any of the books. Jacob looked them all over to see.

One thing that Jacob wanted to do was to find a lame dog that hadn't any place to stay, and was hungry and persecuted, and bring him home and pet him and have that dog's imperishable gratitude. And at last he found one and was happy; and he brought him home and fed him, but when he was going to pet him the dog flew at him and tore all the clothes off him except those that were in front, and made a spectacle of him that was astonishing. He examined authorities, but he could not understand the matter. It was of the same breed of dogs that was in the books, but it acted very differently. Whatever this boy did he got into trouble. The very things the boys in the books got rewarded for turned out to be about the most unprofitable things he could invest in.

Once, when he was on his way to Sunday-school, he saw some bad boys starting off pleasuring in a sailboat. He was filled with consternation, because he knew from his reading that boys who went sailing on Sunday invariably got drowned. So he ran out on a raft to warn them, but a log turned with him and slid him into the river. A man got him out pretty soon, and the doctor pumped the water out of him, and gave him a fresh start with his bellows, but he caught cold and lay sick abed nine weeks. But the most unaccountable thing about it was that the bad boys in the boat had a good time all day, and then reached home alive and well in the most surprising manner. Jacob Blivens said there was nothing like these things in the books. He was perfectly dumfounded.

When he got well he was a little discouraged, but he resolved to keep on trying anyhow. He knew that so far his experiences wouldn't do to go in a book, but he hadn't yet reached the allotted term of life for good little boys, and he hoped to be able to make a record yet if he could hold on till his time was fully up. If everything else failed he had his dying speech to fall back on.

He examined his authorities, and found that it was now time for him to go to sea as a cabin-boy. He called on a ship-captain and made his application, and when the captain asked for his recommendations he proudly drew out a tract and pointed to the word, "To Jacob Blivens, from his affectionate teacher." But the captain was a coarse, vulgar man, and he said, "Oh, that be blowed! that wasn't any proof that he knew how to wash dishes or handle a slush-bucket, and he guessed he didn't want him." This was altogether the most extraordinary thing that ever happened to Jacob in all his life. A compliment from a teacher, on a tract, had never failed to move the tenderest emotions of ship-captains, and open the way to all offices of honor and profit in their gift. He could hardly believe his senses.

This boy always had a hard time of it. Nothing ever came out according to the authorities with him. At last, one day, when he was around hunting up bad little boys to admonish, he found a lot of them in the old iron-foundry fixing up a little joke an fourteen or fifteen dogs, which they had tied together in long procession, and were going to ornament with empty nitroglycerin cans made fast to their tails. Jacob's heart was touched. He sat down on one of those cans ⊠for he never minded grease when duty was before him⊠, and he took hold of the foremost dog by the collar, and turned his reproving eye upon wicked Tom Jones. But just at that moment Alderman McWelter, full of wrath, stepped in. All the bad boys ran away, but Jacob Blivens rose in conscious innocence and began one of those stately little Sunday-school-book speeches which always commence with "Oh, sir!" in dead opposition to the fact that no boy, good or bad, ever starts a remark with "Oh, sir." But the alderman never waited to hear the rest. He took Jacob Blivens by the ear and turned him around, and hit him a whack in the rear with the flat of his hand; and in an instant that good little boy shot out through the roof and soared away toward the sun, with the fragments of those fifteen dogs stringing after him like the tail of a kite. And there wasn't a sign of that alderman or that old iron-foundry left on the face of the earth; and, as for young Jacob Blivens, he never got a chance to make his last dying speech after all his trouble fixing it up, unless he made it to the birds; because, although the bulk of him came down all right in a tree-top in an adjoining county, the rest of him was apportioned around among four townships, and so they had to hold five inquests on him to find out whether he was dead or not, and how it occurred. You never saw a boy scattered so.

Thus perished the good little boy who did the best he could, but didn't come out according to the books. Every boy who ever did as he did prospered except him. His case is truly remarkable. It will probably never be accounted for.

17 威廉·福克納《給愛蜜麗的玫瑰》
——美國南方社會文學小說家

小說特徵

美國南方風土、種族、人情
的寫實

威廉·福克納
(William Faulkner, 1897-1962)

There is no mechanical way to get the writing done, no shortcut. The young writer would be a fool to follow a theory. Teach yourself by your own mistakes; people learn only by error.

-William C. Faulkner

一部作品的完成其實沒有固定方式或捷徑。愚昧的年輕作家只會
服從理論，卻不知從錯誤中學習，自己的錯誤才是良師。

——威廉·福克納

作者短評

　　威廉·福克納（William Cuthbert Faulkner），1897年，生於密西西比州的新奧爾巴尼（New Albany），當他四歲的時候，全家搬到了牛津鎮（Oxford），與馬克·吐溫一樣，從小深受密西西比河的影響，但福克納卻是終生待在美國南方成長、寫作，深受南方傳統風土人情的影響，大多數作品皆以他的故鄉密西西比州為背景，像牛津鎮就是他的小說《給愛蜜麗的玫瑰》中傑佛遜鎮的構想原型。福克納被認為是美國最重要的南方作家之一，他的作品深入刻劃南方歷史、矛盾等敏感問題，生動描繪出南方的風土人文。

　　福克納筆下的劇情浸染著人物的複雜心理變化，綿延婉轉的感情描寫和反復推敲的精巧措詞與海明威簡潔明瞭、乾脆利落的作品風格，是兩個極端。一般認為他是最出色美國現代主義作家，福克納多才多藝，作品範圍廣泛，像他《喧嘩與騷動》（*The Sound and the Fury*）是優秀的意識流作品，但福克納並不是純粹的意識流作家，他的大部分小說創作仍隸屬於寫實主義範疇，他也是多產的短篇小說家，有《給愛蜜麗的玫瑰》、《紅葉》（*Red Leaves*）、《夕陽》（*That Evening Sun*）。1940年，福克納前往好萊塢，一度專著於電影劇本寫作。

　　福克納一生浸泡在酒精之中，即便在1949年，接受諾貝爾文學獎頒贈典禮前，仍喝得酩酊大醉。但他在斯德哥爾摩發表的得獎演說有鑒當時二次大戰甫結束，人類文明屢遭浩劫，一片悲觀時，道出：「我拒絕認為人類已經走到了盡頭……人類能夠忍受艱難困苦，也終將會獲勝」，這席發言和他的性格十分吻合，是諾貝爾文學獎最精彩的感言之一。福克納從1957年起擔任維吉尼亞大學的駐校作家，1959年因騎馬摔下，重傷脊髓，從此苦於傷痛，直到1962年去世，年六十五歲。

作品分析

　　威廉‧福克納《給愛蜜麗的玫瑰》，讀者通常最大疑問就是作者以玫瑰為題，為什麼文章中，卻沒有寫到太多與玫瑰有關連性的內容呢？以福克納對南方獨特的情感與玫瑰高尚不群的優雅特徵，如要將這篇小說的主題與玫瑰作情理聯想，此一玫瑰，當是福克納經由愛蜜麗的生命經歷，象徵性的影射出他所要表達美國南方的不變與不同。

　　愛蜜麗的不幸乃是她對時代的變化，無動於衷，有如帶刺的玫瑰，因此，她拒絕納稅，家中積滿塵埃，連親眼看到父親過逝的事實，也不接受，主題中蘊含了對美國南方傳統、保守固執的遺憾，這一感慨，尤為強烈暗示在愛蜜麗愛上了來自北方到鎮上打工的現代年輕人荷馬，而當荷馬欲棄她而去，愛蜜麗為了保住愛人，竟用砒霜將他毒死，保藏在房中，寧可與代表死亡的荷馬屍體，共枕一生。

　　福克納標題用了玫瑰的意象來描述愛蜜麗的故事，也直接涉及南方女人處境待遇。愛蜜麗出身南方名門，在父親還沒有死之前，被教育的不得拋頭露面，沒有正常的社交，愛蜜麗的父親不只不和鎮上的人連絡，甚至還和親戚朋友斷絕了關係。
這使生活有如在封閉鎖國的愛蜜莉，父親死後，曾經長達有三
天，不相信父親的死去，甚至阻止鎮上的人幫忙。後來她愛
上來自北方的荷馬，也許愛蜜莉所希冀的那朵玫瑰，正是她個
人終於得有一個屬於自己甜蜜的新生花園，在莎士比亞的悲劇
「羅密歐與茱麗葉」裡，當茱麗葉愛上自己家族世仇的羅密歐
時，他懷疑羅密歐的姓名有何意義。她說：「那朵我們稱為玫
瑰的花，若換成別的名字，也是一樣芬芳。」然而這場戀愛，
終究在南方保守風氣，人言可畏下，謠傳北方的荷馬是同性
戀，加上愛蜜麗終究毫無處理愛情的智商下，而宣告破滅，而
在那破滅之後，剩下則是佔有慾望的獨存，可憐愛蜜麗，這朵
被種在溫室的玫瑰呀！

文選閱讀

A Rose for Emily

by William Faulkner

I

When Miss Emily Grierson died, our whole town went to her funeral:
the men through a sort of respectful affection for a fallen monument, the
women mostly out of curiosity to see the inside of her house, which no one

save an old man-servant--a combined gardener and cook--had seen in at least ten years.

It was a big, squarish frame house that had once been white, decorated with cupolas and spires and scrolled balconies in the heavily lightsome style of the seventies, set on what had once been our most select street. But garages and cotton gins had encroached and obliterated even the august names of that neighborhood; only Miss Emily's house was left-- an eyesore among eyesores.

Alive, Miss Emily had been a tradition, a duty, and a care; a sort of hereditary obligation upon the town, dating from that day in 1894 when Colonel Sartoris, the mayor--he who fathered the edict that no Negro woman should appear on the streets without an apron--remitted her taxes, the dispensation dating from the death of her father on into perpetuity. Not that Miss Emily would have accepted charity. Colonel Sartoris invented an involved tale to the effect that Miss Emily's father had loaned money to the town, which the town, as a matter of business, preferred this way of repaying. Only a man of Colonel Sartoris' generation and thought could have invented it, and only a woman could have believed it.

When the next generation, with its more modern ideas, became mayors and aldermen, this arrangement created some little dissatisfaction. On the first of the year they mailed her a tax notice. February came, and there was no reply. They wrote her a formal letter, asking her to call at the sheriff's office at her convenience. A week later the mayor wrote her himself, offering to call or to send his car for her, and received in reply a note on paper of an archaic shape, in a thin, flowing calligraphy in faded ink, to the effect that she no longer went out at all. The tax notice was also enclosed, without comment.

They called a special meeting of the Board of Aldermen. A deputation waited upon her, knocked at the door through which no visitor had passed since she ceased giving china-painting lessons eight or ten years earlier. They were admitted by the old Negro into a dim hall from which a stairway mounted into still more shadow. It smelled of dust and disuse--a close, dank smell. The Negro led them into the parlor. It was furnished in heavy, leather-covered furniture. When the Negro opened the blinds of one window, they could see that the leather was cracked; and when they sat down, a faint dust rose sluggishly about their thighs, spinning with slow motes in the single sun-ray. On a tarnished gilt easel before the fireplace stood a crayon portrait of Miss Emily's father.

They rose when she entered--a small, fat woman in black, with a thin gold chain descending to her waist and vanishing into her belt, leaning on an ebony cane with a tarnished gold head. Her skeleton was small and spare; perhaps that was why what would have been merely plumpness in another was obesity in her. She looked bloated, like a body long submerged in motionless water, and of that pallid hue. Her eyes, lost in the fatty ridges of her face, looked like two small pieces of coal pressed into a lump of dough as they moved from one face to another while the visitors stated their errand.

She did not ask them to sit. She just stood in the door and listened quietly until the spokesman came to a stumbling halt. Then they could hear the invisible watch ticking at the end of the gold chain.

Her voice was dry and cold. "I have no taxes in Jefferson. Colonel Sartoris explained it to me. Perhaps one of you can gain access to the city records and satisfy yourselves."

"But we have. We are the city authorities, Miss Emily. Didn't you get a notice from the sheriff, signed by him?"

"I received a paper, yes," Miss Emily said. "Perhaps he considers himself the sheriff...I have no taxes in Jefferson."

"But there is nothing on the books to show that, you see. We must go by the--"

"See Colonel Sartoris. I have no taxes in Jefferson."

"But, Miss Emily--"

"See Colonel Sartoris." (Colonel Sartoris had been dead almost ten years.) "I have no taxes in Jefferson. Tobe!" The Negro appeared. "Show these gentlemen out."

II

So she vanquished them, horse and foot, just as she had vanquished their fathers thirty years before about the smell. That was two years after her father's death and a short time after her sweetheart--the one we believed would marry her--had deserted her. After her father's death she went out very little; after her sweetheart went away, people hardly saw her at all.

... ,so they were not surprised when the smell developed. ... A neighbor, a woman, complained to the mayor, Judge Stevens, eighty years old.

"But what will you have me do about it, madam?" he said.

"Why, send her word to stop it," the woman said. "Isn't there a law?"

"I'm sure that won't be necessary," Judge Stevens said. "It's probably just a snake or a rat that nigger of hers killed in the yard. I'll speak to him about it."

The next day he received two more complaints, one from a man who came in diffident deprecation. "We really must do something about it, Judge. I'd be the last one in the world to bother Miss Emily, but we've got to do something." That night the Board of Aldermen met--three graybeards and one younger man, a member of the rising generation.

"It's simple enough," he said. "Send her word to have her place cleaned up. Give her a certain time to do it in, and if she don't. . ."

"Dammit, sir," Judge Stevens said, "will you accuse a lady to her face of smelling bad?"

So the next night, after midnight, four men crossed Miss Emily's lawn and slunk about the house like burglars, sniffing along the base of the brickwork and at the cellar openings while one of them performed a regular sowing motion with his hand out of a sack slung from his shoulder. They broke open the cellar door and sprinkled lime there, and in all the outbuildings. As they recrossed the lawn, a window that had been dark was lighted and Miss Emily sat in it, the light behind her, and her upright torso motionless as that of an idol. They crept quietly across the lawn and into the shadow of the locusts that lined the street. After a week or two the smell went away.

That was when people had begun to feel really sorry for her. People in our town, remembering how old lady Wyatt, her great-aunt, had gone completely crazy at last, believed that the Griersons held themselves a little too high for what they really were. None of the young men were quite good enough for Miss Emily and such. We had long thought of them as a tableau, Miss Emily a slender figure in white in the background, her father a spraddled silhouette in the foreground, his back to her and clutching a horsewhip, the two of them framed by the back-flung front door. So when she got to be thirty and was still single, we were not pleased exactly, but vindicated; even with insanity in the family she wouldn't have turned down all of her chances if they had really materialized.

When her father died, it got about that the house was all that was left to her; and in a way, people were glad. At last they could pity Miss Emily. Being left alone, and a pauper, she had become humanized. Now she too would know the old thrill and the old despair of a penny more or less.

The day after his death all the ladies prepared to call at the house and offer condolence and aid, as is our custom Miss Emily met them at the door, dressed as usual and with no trace of grief on her face. She told them that her father was not dead. She did that for three days, with the ministers calling on her, and the doctors, trying to persuade her to let them dispose of the body. Just as they were about to resort to law and force, she broke down, and they buried her father quickly.

We did not say she was crazy then. We believed she had to do that. We remembered all the young men her father had driven away, and we knew that with nothing left, she would have to cling to that which had robbed her, as people will.

III

She was sick for a long time. When we saw her again, her hair was cut short, making her look like a girl, with a vague resemblance to those angels in colored church windows--sort of tragic and serene.

The town had just let the contracts for paving the sidewalks, and in the summer after her father's death they began the work. The construction company came with riggers and mules and machinery, and a foreman named Homer Barron, a Yankee--a big, dark, ready man, with a big voice and eyes lighter than his face. The little boys would follow in groups to hear him cuss the riggers, and the riggers singing in time to the rise and fall of picks. Pretty soon he knew everybody in town. Whenever you heard a lot of laughing anywhere about the square, Homer Barron would be in the center of the group. Presently we began to see him and Miss Emily on Sunday afternoons driving in the yellow-wheeled buggy and the matched team of bays from the livery stable.

At first we were glad that Miss Emily would have an interest, because the ladies all said, "Of course a Grierson would not think seriously of a Northerner, a day laborer." But there were still others, older people, who said that even grief could not cause a real lady to forget *noblesse oblige*--

without calling it *noblesse oblige*…

And as soon as the old people said, "Poor Emily," the whispering began. "Do you suppose it's really so?" they said to one another. "Of course it is. What else could…" This behind their hands; rustling of craned silk and satin behind jalousies closed upon the sun of Sunday afternoon as the thin, swift clop-clop-clop of the matched team passed: "Poor Emily."

She carried her head high enough--even when we believed that she was fallen. It was as if she demanded more than ever the recognition of her dignity as the last Grierson; as if it had wanted that touch of earthiness to reaffirm her imperviousness. Like when she bought the rat poison, the arsenic. That was over a year after they had begun to say "Poor Emily," and while the two female cousins were visiting her.

"I want some poison," she said to the druggist. She was over thirty then, still a slight woman, though thinner than usual, with cold, haughty black eyes in a face the flesh of which was strained across the temples and about the eye-sockets as you imagine a lighthouse-keeper's face ought to look. "I want some poison," she said.

"Yes, Miss Emily. What kind? For rats and such? I'd recom--"

"I want the best you have. I don't care what kind."

The druggist named several. "They'll kill anything up to an elephant. But what you want is--"

"Arsenic," Miss Emily said. "Is that a good one?"

"Is… arsenic? Yes, ma'am. But what you want--"

"I want arsenic."

The druggist looked down at her. She looked back at him, erect, her face like a strained flag. "Why, of course," the druggist said. "If that's what you want. But the law requires you to tell what you are going to use it for."

Miss Emily just stared at him, her head tilted back in order to look him eye for eye, until he looked away and went and got the arsenic and wrapped it up. The Negro delivery boy brought her the package; the druggist didn't come back. When she opened the package at home there was written on the box, under the skull and bones: "For rats."

IV

So the next day we all said, "She will kill herself"; and we said it would be the best thing. When she had first begun to be seen with Homer Barron, we had said, "She will marry him." Then we said, "She will persuade him yet," because Homer himself had remarked--he liked men, and it was known that he drank with the younger men in the Elks' Club--that he was not a marrying man. Later we said, "Poor Emily" behind the jalousies as they passed on Sunday afternoon in the glittering buggy, Miss Emily with her head high and Homer Barron with his hat cocked and a cigar in his teeth, reins and whip in a yellow glove.

Then some of the ladies began to say that it was a disgrace to the town and a bad example to the young people. The men did not want to interfere, but at last the ladies forced the Baptist minister--Miss Emily's people were Episcopal--to call upon her. He would never divulge what happened during that interview, but he refused to go back again. The next Sunday they again drove about the streets, and the following day the minister's wife wrote to Miss Emily's relations in Alabama.

So she had blood-kin under her roof again and we sat back to watch developments. At first nothing happened. Then we were sure that they were to be married. We learned that Miss Emily had been to the jeweler's and ordered a man's toilet set in silver, with the letters H. B. on each piece. Two days later we learned that she had bought a complete outfit of men's clothing, including a nightshirt, and we said, "They are married." We were really glad. We were glad because the two female cousins were even more Grierson than Miss Emily had ever been.

And that was the last we saw of Homer Barron. And of Miss Emily for some time. The Negro man went in and out with the market basket, but the front door remained closed. Now and then we would see her at a window for a moment, as the men did that night when they sprinkled the lime, but for almost six months she did not appear on the streets. Then we knew that this was to be expected too; as if that quality of her father which had thwarted her woman's life so many times had been too virulent and too furious to die.

When we next saw Miss Emily, she had grown fat and her hair was turning gray. During the next few years it grew grayer and grayer until it attained an even pepper-and-salt iron-gray, when it ceased turning. Up to the day of her death at seventy-four it was still that vigorous iron-gray, like the hair of an active man.

From that time on her front door remained closed, save for a period of six or seven years, when she was about forty, during which she gave lessons in china-painting. She fitted up a studio in one of the downstairs rooms, where the daughters and granddaughters of Colonel Sartoris' contemporaries were sent to her with the same regularity and in the same spirit that they were sent to church on Sundays with a twenty-five-cent piece for the collection plate. Meanwhile her taxes had been remitted.

Then the newer generation became the backbone and the spirit of the town, and the painting pupils grew up and fell away and did not send their children to her with boxes of color and tedious brushes and pictures cut from the ladies' magazines. The front door closed upon the last one and remained closed for good. When the town got free postal delivery, Miss Emily alone refused to let them fasten the metal numbers above her door and attach a mailbox to it. She would not listen to them.

Daily, monthly, yearly we watched the Negro grow grayer and more stooped, going in and out with the market basket. Each December we sent her a tax notice, which would be returned by the post office a week later, unclaimed. Now and then we would see her in one of the downstairs windows--she had evidently shut up the top floor of the house--like the carven torso of an idol in a niche, looking or not looking at us, we could never tell which. Thus she passed from generation to generation--dear, inescapable, impervious, tranquil, and perverse.

And so she died. Fell ill in the house filled with dust and shadows, with only a doddering Negro man to wait on her. We did not even know she was sick; we had long since given up trying to get any information from the Negro. He talked to no one, probably not even to her, for his voice had grown harsh and rusty, as if from disuse.

She died in one of the downstairs rooms, in a heavy walnut bed with a curtain, her gray head propped on a pillow yellow and moldy with age and lack of sunlight.

V

The Negro met the first of the ladies at the front door and let them in, with their hushed, sibilant voices and their quick, curious glances, and then he disappeared. He walked right through the house and out the back and was not seen again.

The two female cousins came at once. They held the funeral on the second day, with the town coming to look at Miss Emily beneath a mass of bought flowers, with the crayon face of her father musing profoundly above the bier and the ladies sibilant and macabre; and the very old men-- some in their brushed Confederate uniforms--on the porch and the lawn, talking of Miss Emily as if she had been a contemporary of theirs, believing that they had danced with her and courted her perhaps...

Already we knew that there was one room in that region above stairs which no one had seen in forty years, and which would have to be forced. They waited until Miss Emily was decently in the ground before they opened it.

The violence of breaking down the door seemed to fill this room with pervading dust. A thin, acrid pall as of the tomb seemed to lie everywhere upon this room decked and furnished as for a bridal: upon the valance curtains of faded rose color, upon the rose-shaded lights, upon the dressing table, upon the delicate array of crystal and the man's toilet things backed with tarnished silver, silver so tarnished that the monogram was obscured. Among them lay a collar and tie, as if they had just been removed, which, lifted, left upon the surface a pale crescent in the dust. Upon a chair hung the suit, carefully folded; beneath it the two mute shoes and the discarded socks.

The man himself lay in the bed.

For a long while we just stood there, looking down at the profound and fleshless grin. The body had apparently once lain in the attitude of an embrace, but now the long sleep that outlasts love, that conquers even the grimace of love, had cuckolded him. What was left of him, rotted beneath what was left of the nightshirt, had become inextricable from the bed in which he lay; and upon him and upon the pillow beside him lay that even coating of the patient and biding dust.

Then we noticed that in the second pillow was the indentation of a head. One of us lifted something from it, and leaning forward, that faint and invisible dust dry and acrid in the nostrils, we saw a long strand of iron-gray hair.

18

凱特・蕭邦《一小時的故事》
——美國女性主義小說先驅

小說特徵

美國女性主義與女權

凱特・蕭邦
(Kate Chopin, 1851-1904)

When she abandoned herself a little whispered word escaped her slightly parted lips. She said it over and over under the breath: "free, free, free!"
"Free! Body and soul free!" she kept whispering.

-Kate Chopin, *The Story of An Hour*

當馬勒夫人放空自己，她微張的雙唇，重覆悄聲輕吐「自由、自由、自由！」

「自由！靈魂與肉體的自由！」，她持續低聲說著。

——凱特・蕭邦《一小時的故事》

作者短評

　　凱特・蕭邦（Kate Chopin），本名凱薩琳・歐福拉赫蒂（Katherine O'Flaherty），1851年，生於美國南方路易斯安那，是法國系克里歐人（Creole），蕭邦在作品中處處表達她對女性的關懷，公認為十九世紀美國女性主義作家的先驅。

　　凱特蕭邦超越當時文學傳統和社會風氣紅線，專事女性主義題材寫作，作品著重婦女在事業、婚姻、道德和心理方面的問題，尤其是女性追求自我渴望時所面臨的困境，顛覆了十九世紀美國社會對婦女「三從四德，賢妻良母」的期待與規範。1890年她發表第一部長篇小說《困惑》，是美國最早觸及女性離婚問題的小說。她筆下更試圖描繪出十九世紀女性內心的情慾世界與矛盾不定的心情，作品《暴風雨》（*The Tempest*）赤裸寫出女性在情慾裡體驗到快樂的一面。

　　1899年長篇小說《覺醒》（*Awakening*）出版，此書是凱特最知名的作品，內容是關於一個不滿婚姻生活的妻子，她透過書中的女主角追求自我、愛情、獨立，最後自殺的悲劇，大膽地描寫了婦女自我意識和性意識的覺醒，與美國當時保守氛圍大為衝突，這使蕭邦受到社會長期的冷落、責備，心情沮喪，抑鬱而逝。

　　凱特蕭邦短篇小說中以《一小時的故事》（*The Story of An Hour*）最為經典。隨著六〇年代女權運動興起，被冷落將近半世紀的凱特・蕭邦才又被重新發現，成為美國女性主義文學中的重要作家。

作品分析

筆者上課時，常愛問學生的一個問題就是：美國人和歐洲人，誰比較保守？誰較開放？也許好萊塢電影或美國媒體的強勢，往往大部台灣學生會選擇美國人是較開放的一群，但答案正好相反。因此，在分析凱特・蕭邦的《一個小時的故事》前，除涉及女性在美國社會地位的背景，也正好順帶說明美國民族性的保守。

1776年，美國《獨立宣言》中，最響亮的一句話就是「人生而平等」（All men are created equal.），但其實黑人與女性不在其列；1861年，美國人不惜內戰，犧牲六十萬生命，解放黑奴，1863年，憲法第十三、十四修正案，至少讓黑人在法律上具備與白人同等之公民權利。但女性呢？

二十世紀前，美國女性在社會兩性地位上，可說是隱性到幾乎是隱形了。美國女性地位之卑微與美國清教（Puritans）的傳統大有關係，由霍桑的《紅字》，寫出女人幾乎是男性的附屬品，女人一旦結婚，財產就歸丈夫所有，女性的一生職場就在家庭，最偉大的志業就是養兒育女，相夫教子，稍有見識女子，則視之女巫、異端，而有所謂「獵女巫」（Witch Hunting）事件，殘酷者，以火燒死。也因此，當十九世紀，黑奴都已取得公民地位時，美國女性仍不具有財產、教育及參政權，美國女性是直到1920年時，才得有投票權。美國民族性之保守傾向，即便2004年民主黨的希拉蕊及歐巴馬爭逐總統候選大位時，美國人在面臨第一個女性總統或第一個黑人總統抉擇時，美國人還是寧可選取後者，由此可知，由保守向自由前進一步之維艱！

　　凱特‧蕭邦在《一小時的故事》，敘述馬勒夫人在一個小時中，歷經兩次心情震撼。丈夫火車意外的死訊，讓馬勒夫人帶來「當然」的悲痛，但在剎那之間，馬勒夫人壓抑已久的自我，自然而然近乎潛意識地爆發出來，口中傾吐出：「自由，自由，自由！」，諷刺的是，就在她打算為自己而活，享受如獲重生的喜悅時，丈夫突然返家，她失落絕望之情，導致心臟病發猝死，醫生當場診斷馬勒夫人自是過於高興丈夫生還，才致心臟猝死。

　　凱特蕭邦結局以馬勒夫人的死，而不是以她自主意識的復活勝利為結局，也意謂凱特蕭邦對當時保守道德的牢固與女權發展的悲觀，讓這「一小時的故事」也成了馬勒夫人一生僅有的自由生命。

文選閱讀

The Story of An Hour

by Kate Chopin (1894)

　　Knowing that Mrs. Mallard was afflicted with a heart trouble, great care was taken to break to her as gently as possible the news of her husband's death.

It was her sister Josephine who told her, in broken sentences; veiled hints that revealed in half concealing. Her husband's friend Richards was there, too, near her. It was he who had been in the newspaper office when intelligence of the railroad disaster was received, with Brently Mallard's name leading the list of "killed." He had only taken the time to assure himself of its truth by a second telegram, and had hastened to forestall any less careful, less tender friend in bearing the sad message.

She did not hear the story as many women have heard the same, with a paralyzed inability to accept its significance. She wept at once, with sudden, wild abandonment, in her sister's arms. When the storm of grief had spent itself she went away to her room alone. She would have no one follow her.

There stood, facing the open window, a comfortable, roomy armchair. Into this she sank, pressed down by a physical exhaustion that haunted her body and seemed to reach into her soul.

She could see in the open square before her house the tops of trees that were all aquiver with the new spring life. The delicious breath of rain was in the air. In the street below a peddler was crying his wares. The notes of a distant song which some one was singing reached her faintly, and countless sparrows were twittering in the eaves.

There were patches of blue sky showing here and there through the clouds that had met and piled one above the other in the west facing her window.

She sat with her head thrown back upon the cushion of the chair, quite motionless, except when a sob came up into her throat and shook her, as a child who has cried itself to sleep continues to sob in its dreams.

She was young, with a fair, calm face, whose lines bespoke repression and even a certain strength. But now there was a dull stare in her eyes, whose gaze was fixed away off yonder on one of those patches of blue sky. It was not a glance of reflection, but rather indicated a suspension of intelligent thought.

There was something coming to her and she was waiting for it, fearfully. What was it? She did not know; it was too subtle and elusive to name. But she felt it, creeping out of the sky, reaching toward her through the sounds, the scents, the color that filled the air.

Now her bosom rose and fell tumultuously. She was beginning to recognize this thing that was approaching to possess her, and she was striving to beat it back with her will--as powerless as her two white slender hands would have been. When she abandoned herself a little whispered word escaped her slightly parted lips. She said it over and over under the breath: "free, free, free!" The vacant stare and the look of terror that had followed it went from her eyes. They stayed keen and bright. Her pulses beat fast, and the coursing blood warmed and relaxed every inch of her body.

She did not stop to ask if it were or were not a monstrous joy that held her. A clear and exalted perception enabled her to dismiss the suggestion as trivial. She knew that she would weep again when she saw the kind, tender hands folded in death; the face that had never looked save with love upon her, fixed and gray and dead. But she saw beyond that bitter moment a long procession of years to come that would belong to her absolutely. And she opened and spread her arms out to them in welcome.

There would be no one to live for during those coming years; she would live for herself. There would be no powerful will bending hers in that blind persistence with which men and women believe they have a right to impose a private will upon a fellow-creature. A kind intention or a cruel intention made the act seem no less a crime as she looked upon it in that brief moment of illumination.

And yet she had loved him--sometimes. Often she had not. What did it matter! What could love, the unsolved mystery, count for in the face of this possession of self-assertion which she suddenly recognized as the strongest impulse of her being!

"Free! Body and soul free!" she kept whispering.

Josephine was kneeling before the closed door with her lips to the keyhole, imploring for admission. "Louise, open the door! I beg; open the door--you will make yourself ill. What are you doing, Louise? For heaven's sake open the door."

"Go away. I am not making myself ill." No; she was drinking in a very elixir of life through that open window.

Her fancy was running riot along those days ahead of her. Spring days, and summer days, and all sorts of days that would be her own. She breathed a quick prayer that life might be long. It was only yesterday she had thought with a shudder that life might be long.

She arose at length and opened the door to her sister's importunities. There was a feverish triumph in her eyes, and she carried herself unwittingly like a goddess of Victory. She clasped her sister's waist, and together they descended the stairs. Richards stood waiting for them at the bottom.

Some one was opening the front door with a latchkey. It was Brently Mallard who entered, a little travel-stained, composedly carrying his grip-sack and umbrella. He had been far from the scene of the accident, and did not even know there had been one. He stood amazed at Josephine's piercing cry; at Richards' quick motion to screen him from the view of his wife.

When the doctors came they said she had died of heart disease--of the joy that kills.

19

史考特・費茲傑羅《一個酗酒案例》——美國「失落的一代」與「經濟大恐慌」之代言人

小說特徵

美國「失落的一代」與「經濟大恐慌」之社會現象

史考特・費茲傑羅
(F. Scott Fitzgerald, 1896-1940)

I don't want to repeat my innocence. I want the pleasure of losing it again.

-F. Scott Fitzgerald

與其回復我的純真，我寧可享受再度失去牠的樂趣。

——史考特・費茲傑羅

作者短評

　　史考特・費茲傑羅（F. Scott Fitzgerald），1896年，出生於美國明尼蘇達州的聖保羅市，由於父親經商失敗，只得投靠岳家，過著寄人籬下的生活。大學就讀於普林斯頓大學，1917年從軍，一次大戰結束後，美國進入空前的經濟繁榮，1920年，二十四歲的費茲傑羅首作《塵世樂園》（*This Side of Paradise*）出版後，一夕爆紅，緊接《輕佻女子與哲學家》（*Flappers and Philosophers*）、《爵士時代的故事》（*Tales of the Jazz Age*），都是描述1920年代美國人在歌舞昇平中，產生所謂「失落的一代」（The lost Generation）的空虛、享樂、放浪的社會現象與生活思想。而驟得大名的費茲傑羅也娶了名媛Zelda Sayre為妻，為了維持笙歌宴飲的奢華日子，費滋傑羅開始替《星期六晚郵報》（*Saturday Evening Post*）撰寫了大量連他自己也痛恨的「低俗」（whoring）短篇小說作品，以賺取高額稿酬，這也是為何後世批評他生活腐化、自暴自棄，以致浪費了自己的才華。好時光總是短暫的，緊接而來的三〇年代經濟大恐慌，費滋傑羅飽受妻子精神狀態不佳，以及負債累累的經濟窘困，加上他本身長久以來的酗酒問題，1940年12月22日，聖誕節前夕，費茲傑羅心臟病發作，過世於加州好萊塢公寓，年僅四十四歲。

　　費茲傑羅一生由浮華以至幻滅的起伏歷程，完全重疊與倒映了美國1920年代「失落的一代」富裕下，縱慾與虛空的社會文化及至三〇年代「經濟大恐慌」（The Great Panic）財富破滅的歷程，使他成為這二十個年頭的美國社會與歷史見證，而他的作品也成了編年小說，費茲傑羅最著名的小說為《大亨小傳》（*The Great Gatsby*），堪稱當時美國社會縮影的經典代表。

作品介紹

費茲傑羅用小說方式解讀自己的人生與孕育自己人生的爵士時代（the Jazz Age）——在這個特殊的二〇年代，費茲傑羅已意識到其實金錢才是美國文化中最重要的符號，也是這個符號導致他作品的成功，然而也是這個符號導致了他一生的失敗。費茲傑羅《一個酗酒案例》正是他個人與美國那個多采卻又頹廢，充滿希望又幻滅年代的自剖小說，屬於他人生最末端的作品。他藉由一第三人稱的護士對一酗酒病例的個案觀察，說明酗酒者的沉迷及無奈。最後酗酒的卡通畫家（就是費茲傑羅本人的化身）只有自殺得以解脫，這無奈見於這位護士明知道他要自殺，卻也無濟於事的默許，費茲傑羅濃濃傳達了他難去酒癮的痛楚與他對那個時代的失落感。

費茲傑羅本人自大學時期就染上飲酒習慣，之後酗酒問題愈來愈嚴重，他的早逝與過於沉溺酒精關係甚大。其實，費茲傑羅《一個酗酒案例》與美國當時社會喧騰已久的一段獨特禁酒歷史有關。如前所述，美國1920-30的背景年代，社會步調堪稱是雲霄飛車的時代，先是一戰後的經濟過熱，紙醉金迷的生活隨之而來，之後，經濟大恐慌，股市慘跌，又千金散去，不少人以跳樓自殺，結束生命，但有樣東西，在這期間卻是死而復生，就是酒。美國人是以「清教」立國，禁慾、簡約是傳統生活原則，酒老早看成是犯罪、家暴和貧窮的根源，社會改革運動人士早極欲去之而後快，一戰後，生活的糜爛氛圍，終於在民氣可用之下，禁酒被提升至國家意志的高度，在1919年，美國憲法第十八修正案使美國成為禁酒的國家，但這實在也是美國史上最愚蠢的法案，因為，沒有任何東西能夠改造人性，政府可以用法律宣佈酒類為禁品，但卻不可能從人的心中清除喝酒的慾望，1933年，美國在經濟大恐慌下，羅斯福以憲法第十九條修正案撤銷禁酒令，讓苦悶的人民至少有酒澆愁。費茲傑羅除了表達個人酗酒的無奈，也間接的表現了禁酒好比要人民不要抽煙一樣的天真。

文選閱讀

An Alcoholic Case

by F. Scott Fitzgerald

"Let--go--that--Oh-h-h! Please, now, will you? Don't start drinking again! Come on--give me the bottle. I told you I'd stay awake givin' it to you. Come on. Come on--leave it with me--I'll leave half in the bottle. Pul-lease. *You know what Dr Carter says, I'm too tired to be fightin' you all night... All right, drink your fool self to death.*"

"Would you like some beer?" he asked.

"No, I don't want any beer. Oh, to think that I have to look at you drunk again. My God!"

"Then I'll drink the Coca Cola."

"Don't you believe in anything?" she demanded.

"Nothing you believe in--please--it'll spill."

Again they struggled, but after this time he sat with his head in his hands awhile, before he turned around once more.

"Once more you try to get it I'll throw it down," she said quickly. "I will--on the tiles in the bathroom."

"Then I'll step on the broken glass--or you'll step on it."

"Then let go--oh you promised--"

Suddenly she dropped it like a torpedo, sliding underneath her hand and slithering with a flash of red and black and the words: SIR GALAHAD, DISTILLED LOUISVILLE GIN through the open door to the bathroom.

It was on the floor in pieces and everything was silent for a while. She began to worry that he would have to go into the bathroom and might cut his feet, and looked up from time to time to see if he would go in. She was very sleepy--the last time she looked up he was crying and he looked like an old Jewish man she had nursed once in California; he had had to go to the bathroom many times. On this case she was unhappy all the time but she thought:

"I guess if I hadn't liked him I wouldn't have stayed on the case."

With a sudden resurgence of conscience she got up and put a chair in front of the bathroom door. She had wanted to sleep because he had got her up early that morning and she hadn't been home all day. That afternoon a relative of his had come to see him and she had waited outside in the hall where there was a draught with no sweater to put over her uniform.

As well as she could she arranged him for sleeping, put a robe over his shoulders as he sat slumped over his writing table, and one on his knees.

She sat down in the rocker but she was no longer sleepy; there was plenty to enter on the chart and she found a pencil and put it down:

Pulse 120

Respiration 25

Temp. 98--98.4--98.2

Remarks--

--She could make so many:

Tried to get bottle of gin. Threw it away and broke it.

She corrected it to read:

In the struggle it dropped and was broken. Patient was generally difficult.

She started to add as part of her report: *I never want to go on an alcoholic case again*, but that wasn't in the picture. She knew she could wake herself at seven and clean up everything before his niece awakened. It was all part of the game. But when she sat down in the chair she looked at his face, white and exhausted, and counted his breathing again, wondering why it had all happened. He had been so nice today, drawn her a whole strip of his cartoon just for fun and given it to her. She was going to have it framed and hang it in her room. She felt again his thin wrists wrestling against her wrist and remembered the awful things he had said, and she thought too of what the doctor had said to him yesterday:

'You're too good a man to do this to yourself.'

She was tired and didn't want to clean up the glass on the bathroom floor, because as soon as he breathed evenly she wanted to get him over to the bed. But she decided finally to clean up the glass first; on her knees, searching a last piece of it, she thought:

--This isn't what I ought to be doing. And this isn't what he ought to be doing.

The glass was all collected--as she got out a broom to make sure, she realized that the glass, in its fragments, was less than a window through which they had seen each other for a moment…It was so utterly senseless--as she put a bandage on her finger where she had cut it while picking up the glass she made up her mind she would never take an alcoholic case again.

It was early the next evening. Some Halloween jokester had split the side windows of the bus and she shifted back to the Negro section in the rear for fear the glass might fall out. She had her patient's cheque but no way to cash it at this hour; there was a quarter and a penny in her purse.

Two nurses she knew were waiting in the hall of Mrs Hixson's Agency.

"What kind of case have you been on?"

"Alcoholic," she said.

"Oh, yes--Gretta Hawks told me about it--you were on with that cartoonist who lives at the Forest Park Inn."

"Yes, I was."

"I hear he's pretty fresh."

"He's never done anything to bother me," she lied.

In a moment Mrs. Hixson came out and, asking the other two to wait, signaled her into the office.

"I got your call from the hotel.'", she began.

"Oh, it wasn't bad, Mrs Hixson. He didn't know what he was doing and he didn't hurt me in any way. I was thinking much more of my reputation with you. He was really nice all day yesterday. He drew me--"

"I didn't want to send you on that case." Mrs Hixson thumbed through the registration cards. "You take T.B. cases, don't you? Yes, I see you do. Now here's one--"

The phone rang in a continuous chime. The nurse listened as Mrs Hixson's voice said precisely:

"I will do what I can--that is simply up to the doctor…That is beyond my jurisdiction…Oh, hello, Hattie, no, I can't now. *Look, have you got any nurse that's good with alcoholics? There's somebody up at the Forest Park Inn who needs somebody.* Call back will you?"

She put down the receiver. "Suppose you wait outside. What sort of man is this, anyhow? Did he act indecently?"

"He held my hand away," she said, "so I couldn't give him an injection."

"Oh, an invalid he-man," Mrs Hixson grumbled. "They belong in sanatoria. I've got a case coming along in two minutes that you can get a little rest on. It's an old woman--"

The phone rang again. "Oh, hello, Hattie...Well, how about that big Svensen girl? She ought to be able to take care of any alcoholic...How about Josephine Markham? Doesn't she live in your apartment house? ...Get her to the phone." Then after a moment, "Joe, would you care to take the case of a well-known cartoonist, or artist, whatever they call themselves, at Forest Park Inn?. .. No, I don't know, but Dr Carter is in charge and will be around about ten o'clock."

Mrs. Hixson hung up the receiver and made notations on the pad before her. She was a very efficient woman. She had been a nurse and had gone through the worst of it, ... She swung around suddenly from the desk.

"What kind of cases do you want? I told you I have a nice old woman--"

The nurse's brown eyes were alight with a mixture of thoughts--the movie she had just seen about Pasteur and the book they had all read about Florence Nightingale when they were student nurses. And their pride, swinging across the streets in the cold weather at Philadelphia General, as proud of their new capes as débutantes in their furs going into balls at the hotels.

"I--I think I would like to try the case again," she said amid a cacophony of telephone bells. "I'd just as soon go back if you can't find anybody else."

"But one minute you say you'll never go on an alcoholic case again and the next minute you say you want to go back to one."

"I think I overestimated how difficult it was. Really, I think I could help him."

"That's up to you. But if he tried to grab your wrists."

"But he couldn't," the nurse said. "Look at my wrists: I played basketball at Waynesboro High for two years. I'm quite able to take care of him."

Mrs. Hixson looked at her for a long minute. "Well, all right," she said. "But just remember that nothing they say when they're drunk is what they mean when they're sober--I've been all through that; arrange with one of the servants that you can call on him, because you never can tell--some alcoholics are pleasant and some of them are not, but all of them can be rotten."

"I'll remember," the nurse said.

It was an oddly clear night when she went out, with slanting particles of thin sleet making white of a blue-black sky. The bus was the same that had taken her into town, but there seemed to be more windows broken now and the bus driver was irritated and talked about what terrible things he would do if he caught any kids. She knew he was just talking about the annoyance in general, just as she had been thinking about the annoyance of an alcoholic. When she came up to the suite and found him all helpless and distraught she would despise him and be sorry for him.

Getting off the bus, she went down the long steps to the hotel, feeling a little exalted by the chill in the air. She was going to take care of him because nobody else would, and because the best people of her profession had been interested in taking care of the cases that nobody else wanted.

She knocked at his study door, knowing just what she was going to say.

He answered it himself. He was in dinner clothes even to a derby hat--but minus his studs and tie.

"Oh, hello," he said casually. "Glad you're back. I woke up a while ago and decided I'd go out. Did you get a night nurse?"

"I'm the night nurse too," she said. "I decided to stay on twenty-four-hour duty."

He broke into a genial, indifferent smile.

"I thought you had quit me," he said casually.

"I thought I had, too."

"If you look on that table," he said, "you'll find a whole strip of cartoons that I drew you."

"Who are you going to see?" she asked.

"It's the President's secretary," he said. "I had an awful time trying to get ready. I was about to give up when you came in. Will you order me some sherry?"

"One glass," she agreed wearily...

"You'll come up soon?" she asked. "Dr Carter's coming at ten."

"What nonsense! You're coming down with me."

"Me?" she exclaimed.

"Then I won't go."

"All right then, go to bed. That's where you belong anyhow. Can't you see these people tomorrow?"

"No, of course not!"

She went behind him and reaching over his shoulder tied his tie--his shirt was already thumbed out of press where he had put in the studs, and she suggested:

"Won't you put on another one, if you've got to meet some people you like?"

"All right, but I want to do it myself."

"Why can't you let me help you?" she demanded in exasperation. "Why can't you let me help you with your clothes? What's a nurse for-- what good am I doing?"

He sat down suddenly on the toilet seat.

"All right--go on."

"Now don't grab my wrist," she said, and then, "Excuse me."

"Don't worry. It didn't hurt. You'll see in a minute."

…he dragged at his cigarette…delaying her.

"Now watch this," he said. "One--two--three."

She pulled up the undershirt; simultaneously he thrust the crimson-grey point of the cigarette like a dagger against his heart. It crushed out against a copper plate on his left rib about the size of a silver dollar, and he said "Ouch!" as a stray spark fluttered down against his stomach.

Now was the time to be hard-boiled, she thought. She knew there were three medals from the war in his jewel box, but she had risked many things herself: tuberculosis among them and one time something worse, though she had not known it and had never quite forgiven the doctor for not telling her.

"You've had a hard time with that, I guess," she said lightly as she sponged him. "Won't it ever heal?"

"Never. That's a copper plate."

"Well, It's no excuse for what you're doing to yourself."

He bent his great brown eyes on her, shrewd--aloof, confused. He signaled to her, in one second, his Will to Die, and for all her training and experience she knew she could never do anything constructive with him. He stood up, steadying himself on the wash-basin and fixing his eyes on some place just ahead.

"Now, if I'm going to stay here you're not going to get at that liquor," she said. Suddenly she knew he wasn't looking for that. He was looking at the corner where he had thrown the bottle the night before. She stared at his handsome face, weak and defiant--afraid to turn even half-way because she knew that death was in that corner where he was looking. She knew death--she had heard it, smelt its unmistakable odour, but she had never seen it before it entered into anyone, and she knew this man saw it in the corner of his bathroom; that it was standing there looking at him.

She tried to express it next day to Mrs Hixson: "It's not like anything you can beat--no matter how hard you try. This one could have twisted my wrists until he strained them and that wouldn't matter so much to me. It's just that you can't really help them and It's so discouraging--It's all for nothing."

薛吾德·安德森《林中之死》
——生與死的奧秘美學

薛吾德·安德森
(Sherwood Anderson, 1876-1941)

A thing so complete has its own beauty.

-Sherwood Anderson

一件如此完整的事情必有其美麗。

——薛吾德·安德森

作者短評

薛吾德・安德森（Sherwood Anderson），1876年，生於美國俄亥俄州，父親經商失敗，酗酒過世後，從此漂流不定，十四歲的安德森只能到處工作，挑起支撐家庭擔子。

薛吾德・安德森之後從軍、念大學，結婚、生子，眼看幸福生活到來時，1912年，安德森精神崩潰，拋家棄子，回到芝加哥，決心進行寫作生涯。1919年，安德森出版《小城畸人》（*Winesburg, Ohio*），一炮而紅，他在書中羅列著上百個人世間之謂「真理」——有童貞與慾望、節儉與放蕩、健康與財富、冷漠與自棄等價值觀。安德森以為正是這些真理使人變成「畸形」，《小城畸人》表達了安德森濃厚的鄉村主義和懷舊情節，流露出安德森反工業文明和資本主義倫理的思想，開創了「芝加哥文藝復興」（Chicago literary renaissance, 1912-1925）學派，對美國二十世紀重要作家福克納、海明威、史坦貝克等人，皆有重要的影響，是美國文學史上重要的起承人物。但薛吾德・安德森從此卻糾纏於婚姻——安德森一生結婚四次——的離合之中，作品也大不如前，深受他影響的海明威，就不止一次為安德森感到遺憾。

1941年，薛吾德・安德森在巴拿馬過逝，年64。在他埋骨所在的維吉尼亞，墓碑上刻寫「生命，而非死亡，才是偉大的冒險」（Life, Not Death, is the Great Adventure）。

　　薛吾德・安德森《林中之死》是由第一人稱的敘事者，重述一件蘊積多年，小時候發生的故事，文中所爭的不是那一個才是事情真相的版本，而是自述者所謂的「一件完整的事情，必有其美麗」，表達作者企圖了解生命與死亡的奧秘，找尋人在每天平凡生活中的美麗與意義。

　　薛吾德・安德森擅用人事的畸形，來表現工業社會這群畸人內心所造成的創傷，這些作品側重自心理角度，表現現代生活中的怪誕和病態，安德森在對女人描述時，傾注了特別的關注與同情。《林中之死》是敘事者根據他個人的經驗去附會事實，來紀錄他童年時候，對一位老太太的記憶，她一生坎坷，晚景淒涼，自出生作人養女被虐待，到遇人不淑，丈夫、兒子稍有不順，動輒對她打罵，平常，靠著賣雞蛋換取食物，只有鎮上的屠夫願意跟她講話，順帶奉送一些內臟、骨頭作為她的餵狗食物，她一生的過程就是不停地餵食主人、丈夫、兒子與一大群的狗、牛，而毫無怨言。一天，她週而復始的帶著她的狗群，去鎮上用蛋換取食物，並取得屠夫較以往更豐富的奉贈，在返回家中的路上，她改走了林中小徑，在石上坐下來休息的時候，安靜的過逝，她的狗群，這時「已不再是狗，而回復狼」，有如儀式般圍繞著她奔跑，當獵人發現她屍體時，「看起來是那麼白皙、可愛，有如大理石，狹小的肩軀，在死亡時，宛如少女的美麗身體」，死亡與美麗反畫上了等號。

《林中之死》是安德森暗示回憶是藝術題材滋生的寶庫，記憶中的靜態景象或畫面亦屬藝術表現之泉源，《林中之死》自述人在真實的題材中，以他童年漫不經心的記憶開始，經過長年的想像與體認老太太遭遇的縈繞心弦，到最後，他把自己成年後的事情也連在一起，這使得兩人之間的連鎖關係成立，自述者在透過經驗與想像力認識「別人的我」，從而找到「自我」的意義，促成了一篇結構完美藝術品的產生是安德森的美學典型之作。

文選閱讀

Death In The Woods

by Sherwood Anderson

I

　　She was an old woman and lived on a farm near the town in which I lived. All country and small-town people have seen such old women, but no one knows much about them. Such an old woman comes into town driving an old worn-out horse or she comes afoot carrying a basket. She may own a few hens and have eggs to sell. She brings them in a basket and takes them to a grocer. There she trades them in. She gets some salt pork and some beans. Then she gets a pound or two of sugar and some flour.

Afterwards she goes to the butcher's and asks for some dog-meat. She may spend ten or fifteen cents, but when she does she asks for something. Formerly the butchers gave liver to any one who wanted to carry it away. In our family we were always having it. Once one of my brothers got a whole cow's liver at the slaughter-house near the fairgrounds in our town. We had it until we were sick of it. It never cost a cent. I have hated the thought of it ever since.

The old farm woman got some liver and a soup-bone. She never visited with any one, and as soon as she got what she wanted she lit out for home. It made quite a load for such an old body. No one gave her a lift. People drive right down a road and never notice an old woman like that.

The old woman was nothing special. She was one of the nameless ones that hardly any one knows, but she got into my thoughts. I have just suddenly now, after all these years, remembered her and what happened. It is a story. Her name was Grimes, and she lived with her husband and son in a small unpainted house on the bank of a small creek four miles from town.

The husband and son were a tough lot. Although the son was but twenty-one, he had already served a term in jail. It was whispered about that the woman's husband stole horses. Now and then, when a horse turned up missing, the man had also disappeared. No one ever caught him. ... The old man belonged to a family that had had money once. His name was Jake Grimes. His father, John Grimes, had owned a sawmill when the country was new, and had made money. Then he got to drinking and running after women. When he died there wasn't much left.

Jake blew in the rest. Pretty soon there wasn't any more lumber to cut and his land was nearly all gone.

He got his wife off a German farmer, for whom he went to work one June day in the wheat harvest. He got her pretty easy himself, the first time he was out with her. He wouldn't have married her if the German farmer hadn't tried to tell him where to get off. He got her to go riding with him in his buggy one night when he was threshing on the place, and then he came for her the next Sunday night.

She managed to get out of the house without her employer's seeing, but when she was getting into the buggy he showed up. It was almost dark, and he just popped up suddenly at the horse's head. He grabbed the horse by the bridle and Jake got out his buggy-whip.

They had it out all right! The German was a tough one. Maybe he didn't care whether his wife knew or not. Jake hit him over the face and shoulders with the buggy-whip, but the horse got to acting up and he had to get out.

Then the two men went for it. The girl didn't see it. The horse started to run away and went nearly a mile down the road before the girl got him stopped. Then she managed to tie him to a tree beside the road. Jake found her there after he got through with the German. She was huddled up in the buggy seat, crying, scared to death. She told Jake a lot of stuff, how the German had tried to get her, how he chased her once into the barn, how another time, when they happened to be alone in the house together, he tore her dress open clear down the front. The German, she said, might have got her that time if he hadn't heard his old woman drive in at the gate. She had been off to town for supplies. Well, she would be putting the horse in the barn. The German managed to sneak off to the fields without his wife seeing. He told the girl he would kill her if she told. What could she do? She told a lie about ripping her dress in the barn when she was feeding the stock. I remember now that she was a bound girl and did not know where her father and mother were. Maybe she did not have any father. You know what I mean.

Such bound children were often enough cruelly treated. They were children who had no parents, slaves really. There were very few orphan homes then. They were legally bound into some home. It was a matter of pure luck how it came out.

II

She married Jake and had a son and daughter, but the daughter died.

Then she settled down to feed stock. That was her job. At the German's place she had cooked the food for the German and his wife. The wife was a strong woman with big hips and worked most of the time in the fields with her husband. She fed them and fed the cows in the barn, fed the pigs, the horses and the chickens. Every moment of every day, as a young girl, was spent feeding something.

Then she married Jake Grimes and he had to be fed. She was a slight thing, and when she had been married for three or four years, and after the two children were born, her slender shoulders became stooped.

Jake always had a lot of big dogs around the house, that stood near the unused sawmill near the creek. He was always trading horses when he wasn't stealing something and had a lot of poor bony ones about. Also he kept three or four pigs and a cow. They were all pastured in the few acres left of the Grimes place and Jake did little enough work.

He went into debt for a threshing outfit and ran it for several years, but it did not pay. People did not trust him. They were afraid he would steal the grain at night. He had to go a long way off to get work and it cost too much to get there. In the Winter he hunted and cut a little firewood, to be sold in some nearby town. When the son grew up he was just like the father. They got drunk together. If there wasn't anything to eat in the house when they came home the old man gave his old woman a cut over the head. She had a few chickens of her own and had to kill one of them in a hurry. When they were all killed she wouldn't have any eggs to sell when she went to town, and then what would she do?

She had to scheme all her life about getting things fed, getting the pigs fed so they would grow fat and could be butchered in the Fall. When they were butchered her husband took most of the meat off to town and sold it. If he did not do it first the boy did. They fought sometimes and when they fought the old woman stood aside trembling.

She had got the habit of silence anyway--that was fixed. Sometimes, when she began to look old--she wasn't forty yet--and when the husband and son were both off, trading horses or drinking or hunting or stealing, she went around the house and the barnyard muttering to herself.

How was she going to get everything fed?--that was her problem. The dogs had to be fed. There wasn't enough hay in the barn for the horses and the cow. If she didn't feed the chickens how could they lay eggs? Without eggs to sell how could she get things in town, things she had to have to keep the life of the farm going? Thank heaven, she did not have to feed her husband--in a certain way. That hadn't lasted long after their marriage and after the babies came. Where he went on his long trips she did not know. Sometimes he was gone from home for weeks, and after the boy grew up they went off together.

They left everything at home for her to manage and she had no money. She knew no one. No one ever talked to her in town. When it was Winter she had to gather sticks of wood for her fire, had to try to keep the stock fed with very little grain.

The stock in the barn cried to her hungrily, the dogs followed her about. In the Winter the hens laid few enough eggs. They huddled in the corners of the barn and she kept watching them. If a hen lays an egg in the barn in the Winter and you do not find it, it freezes and breaks.

One day in Winter the old woman went off to town with a few eggs and the dogs followed her. She did not get started until nearly three o'clock and the snow was heavy. She hadn't been feeling very well for several days and so she went muttering along, scantily clad, her shoulders stooped. She had an old grain bag in which she carried her eggs, tucked away down in the bottom. There weren't many of them, but in Winter the price of eggs is up. She would get a little meat in exchange for the eggs, some salt pork, a little sugar, and some coffee perhaps. It might be the butcher would give her a piece of liver.

When she had got to town and was trading in her eggs the dogs lay by the door outside. She did pretty well, got the things she needed, more than she had hoped. Then she went to the butcher and he gave her some liver and some dog-meat.

It was the first time any one had spoken to her in a friendly way for a long time. The butcher was alone in his shop when she came in and was annoyed by the thought of such a sick-looking old woman out on such a day. It was bitter cold and the snow, that had let up during the afternoon, was falling again. The butcher said something about her husband and her son, swore at them, and the old woman stared at him, a look of mild surprise in her eyes as he talked. He said that if either the husband or the son were going to get any of the liver or the heavy bones with scraps of meat hanging to them that he had put into the grain bag, he'd see him starve first.

Starve, eh? Well, things had to be fed. Men had to be fed, and the horses that weren't any good but maybe could be traded off, and the poor thin cow that hadn't given any milk for three months.

Horses, cows, pigs, dogs, men.

III

The old woman had to get back before darkness came if she could. The dogs followed at her heels, sniffing at the heavy grain bag she had fastened on her back. When she got to the edge of town she stopped by a fence and tied the bag on her back with a piece of rope she had carried in her dress-pocket for just that purpose. That was an easier way to carry it. Her arms ached. It was hard when she had to crawl over fences and once she fell over and landed in the snow. The dogs went frisking about. She had to struggle to get to her feet again, but she made it. The point of climbing over the fences was that there was a short cut over a hill and through a woods. She might have gone around by the road, but it was a mile farther that way. She was afraid she couldn't make it. And then, besides, the stock had to be fed. There was a little hay left and a little corn. Perhaps her husband and son would bring some home when they came. They were going to trade horses, get a little money if they could. They might come home drunk. It would be well to have something in the house when they came back.

The son had an affair on with a woman at the county seat, fifteen miles away. She was a rough enough woman, a tough one. Once, in the Summer, the son had brought her to the house. Both she and the son had been drinking. Jake Grimes was away and the son and his woman ordered the old woman about like a servant. She didn't mind much; she was used to it. Whatever happened she never said anything. That was her way of getting along. She had managed that way when she was a young girl at the German's and ever since she had married Jake. That time her son brought his woman to the house they stayed all night, sleeping together just as though they were married. It hadn't shocked the old woman, not much. She had got past being shocked early in life.

With the pack on her back she went painfully along across an open field, wading in the deep snow, and got into the woods.

There was a path, but it was hard to follow. Just beyond the top of the hill, where the woods was thickest, there was a small clearing. Had some one once thought of building a house there? The clearing was as large as a building lot in town, large enough for a house and a garden. The path ran along the side of the clearing, and when she got there the old woman sat down to rest at the foot of a tree.

It was a foolish thing to do. When she got herself placed, the pack against the tree's trunk, it was nice, but what about getting up again? She worried about that for a moment and then quietly closed her eyes.

She must have slept for a time. When you are about so cold you can't get any colder. The afternoon grew a little warmer and the snow came thicker than ever. Then after a time the weather cleared. The moon even came out.

There were four Grimes dogs that had followed Mrs. Grimes into town, all tall gaunt fellows. Such men as Jake Grimes and his son always keep just such dogs. They kick and abuse them, but they stay. The Grimes dogs, in order to keep from starving, had to do a lot of foraging for themselves, and they had been at it while the old woman slept with her back to the tree at the side of the clearing. They had been chasing rabbits in the woods and in adjoining fields and in their ranging had picked up three other farm dogs.

The dogs in the clearing, before the old woman, had caught two or three rabbits and their immediate hunger had been satisfied. They began to play, running in circles in the clearing. Round and round they ran, each dog's nose at the tail of the next dog. In the clearing, under the snow-laden trees and under the wintry moon they made a strange picture, running thus silently, in a circle their running had beaten in the soft snow. The dogs made no sound. They ran around and around in the circle.

It may have been that the old woman saw them doing that before she died. She may have awakened once or twice and looked at the strange sight with dim old eyes.

She wouldn't be very cold now, just drowsy. Life hangs on a long time.

Perhaps the old woman was out of her head. She may have dreamed of her girlhood, at the German's, and before that, when she was a child and before her mother lit out and left her.

Her dreams couldn't have been very pleasant. Not many pleasant things had happened to her. Now and then one of the Grimes dogs left the running circle and came to stand before her. The dog thrust his face close to her face. His red tongue was hanging out.

The running of the dogs may have been a kind of death ceremony. It may have been that the primitive instinct of the wolf, having been aroused in the dogs by the night and the running, made them somehow afraid.

"Now we are no longer wolves. We are dogs, the servants of men. Keep alive, man! When man dies we becomes wolves again."

The old woman died softly and quietly. When she was dead and when one of the Grimes dogs had come to her and had found her dead all the dogs stopped running.

They gathered about her.

Well, she was dead now. She had fed the Grimes dogs when she was alive, what about now?

There was the pack on her back, the grain bag containing the piece of salt pork, the liver the butcher had given her, the dog-meat, the soup bones. The butcher in town, having been suddenly overcome with a feeling of pity, had loaded her grain bag heavily. It had been a big haul for the old woman.

It was a big haul for the dogs now.

IV

One of the Grimes dogs sprang suddenly out from among the others and began worrying the pack on the old woman's back. Had the dogs really been wolves that one would have been the leader of the pack. What he did, all the others did.

All of them sank their teeth into the grain bag the old woman had fastened with ropes to her back.

They dragged the old woman's body out into the open clearing. The worn-out dress was quickly torn from her shoulders. When she was found, a day or two later, the dress had been torn from her body clear to the hips, but the dogs had not touched her body. They had got the meat out of the grain bag, that was all. Her body was frozen stiff when it was found, and the shoulders were so narrow and the body so slight that in death it looked like the body of some charming young girl.

Such things happened in towns of the Middle West, on farms near town, when I was a boy. A hunter out after rabbits found the old woman's body and did not touch it. Something, the beaten round path in the little snow-covered clearing, the silence of the place, the place where the dogs had worried the body trying to pull the grain bag away or tear it open-- something startled the man and he hurried off to town.

I was in Main street with one of my brothers who was town newsboy and who was taking the afternoon papers to the stores. It was almost night.

The hunter came into a grocery and told his story. Then he went to a hardware-shop and into a drugstore. Men began to gather on the sidewalks. Then they started out along the road to the place in the woods.

My brother should have gone on about his business of distributing papers but he didn't. Every one was going to the woods. The undertaker went and the town marshal. Several men got on a dray and rode out to where the path left the road and went into the woods, but the horses weren't very sharply shod and slid about on the slippery roads. They made no better time than those of us who walked.

The town marshal was a large man whose leg had been injured in the Civil War. He carried a heavy cane and limped rapidly along the road. My brother and I followed at his heels, and as we went other men and boys joined the crowd.

It had grown dark by the time we got to where the old woman had left the road but the moon had come out. The marshal was thinking there might have been a murder. He kept asking the hunter questions. The hunter went along with his gun across his shoulders, a dog following at his heels. It isn't often a rabbit hunter has a chance to be so conspicuous. He was taking full advantage of it, leading the procession with the town marshal. "I didn't see any wounds. She was a beautiful young girl. Her face was buried in the snow. No, I didn't know her." As a matter of fact, the hunter had not looked closely at the body. He had been frightened. She might have been murdered and some one might spring out from behind a tree and murder him. In a woods, in the late afternoon, when the trees are all bare and there is white snow on the ground, when all is silent, something creepy steals over the mind and body. If something strange or uncanny has happened in the neighborhood all you think about is getting away from there as fast as you can.

The crowd of men and boys had got to where the old woman had crossed the field and went, following the marshal and the hunter, up the slight incline and into the woods.

Now the crowd of men and boys had got to the clearing. Darkness comes quickly on such Winter nights, but the full moon made everything clear. My brother and I stood near the tree, beneath which the old woman had died.

She did not look old, lying there in that light, frozen and still. One of the men turned her over in the snow and I saw everything. My body trembled with some strange mystical feeling and so did my brother's. It might have been the cold.

Neither of us had ever seen a woman's body before. It may have been the snow, clinging to the frozen flesh, that made it look so white and lovely, so like marble. No woman had come with the party from town; but one of the men, he was the town blacksmith, took off his overcoat and spread it over her. Then he gathered her into his arms and started off to town, all the others following silently. At that time no one knew who she was.

<h2 style="text-align:center">V</h2>

I had seen everything, had seen the oval in the snow, like a miniature race-track, where the dogs had run, had seen how the men were mystified, had seen the white bare young-looking shoulders, had heard the whispered comments of the men.

The men were simply mystified. They took the body to the undertaker's, and when the blacksmith, the hunter, the marshal and several others had got inside they closed the door. If father had been there perhaps he could have got in, but we boys couldn't.

I went with my brother to distribute the rest of his papers and when we got home it was my brother who told the story.

I kept silent and went to bed early. It may have been I was not satisfied with the way he told it.

Later, in the town, I must have heard other fragments of the old woman's story. She was recognized the next day and there was an investigation.

The husband and son were found somewhere and brought to town and there was an attempt to connect them with the woman's death, but it did not work. They had perfect enough alibis.

However, the town was against them. They had to get out. Where they went I never heard.

I remember only the picture there in the forest, the men standing about, the naked girlish-looking figure, face down in the snow, the tracks made by the running dogs and the clear cold Winter sky above. White fragments of clouds were drifting across the sky. They went racing across the little open space among the trees.

The scene in the forest had become for me, without my knowing it, the foundation for the real story I am now trying to tell. The fragments, you see, had to be picked up slowly, long afterwards.

The whole thing, the story of the old woman's death, was to me as I grew older like music heard from far off. The notes had to be picked up slowly one at a time. Something had to be understood.

The woman who died was one destined to feed animal life. Anyway, that is all she ever did. She was feeding animal life before she was born, as a child, as a young woman working on the farm of the German, after she married, when she grew old and when she died. She fed animal life in cows, in chickens, in pigs, in horses, in dogs, in men. Her daughter had died in childhood and with her one son she had no articulate relations. On the night when she died she was hurrying homeward, bearing on her body food for animal life.

She died in the clearing in the woods and even after her death continued feeding animal life.

You see it is likely that, when my brother told the story, that night when we got home and my mother and sister sat listening, I did not think he got the point. He was too young and so was I. A thing so complete has its own beauty.

I shall not try to emphasize the point. I am only explaining why I was dissatisfied then and have been ever since. I speak of that only that you may understand why I have been impelled to try to tell the simple story over again.

語言文學類　PG0806

人性深邃之拜訪
──美國近代經典短篇小說選

編　　著/涂成吉
責任編輯/陳佳怡
圖文排版/張慧雯
封面設計/蔡瑋中

發　行　人/宋政坤
法律顧問/毛國樑　律師
印製出版/秀威資訊科技股份有限公司
　　　　　114台北市內湖區瑞光路76巷65號1樓
　　　　　電話：+886-2-2796-3638　傳真：+886-2-2796-1377
　　　　　http://www.showwe.com.tw
劃撥帳號/19563868　戶名：秀威資訊科技股份有限公司
　　　　　讀者服務信箱：service@showwe.com.tw
展售門市/國家書店（松江門市）
　　　　　104台北市中山區松江路209號1樓
　　　　　電話：+886-2-2518-0207　傳真：+886-2-2518-0778
網路訂購/秀威網路書店：http://www.bodbooks.com.tw
　　　　　國家網路書店：http://www.govbooks.com.tw
圖書經銷/紅螞蟻圖書有限公司
　　　　　114台北市內湖區舊宗路二段121巷28、32號4樓
　　　　　電話：+886-2-2795-3656　傳真：+886-2-2795-4100

2012年9月BOD一版
定價：300元
版權所有　翻印必究
本書如有缺頁、破損或裝訂錯誤，請寄回更換

國家圖書館出版品預行編目

人性深邃之拜訪：美國近代經典短篇小說選 / 涂成吉編著. --
　一版. -- 臺北市：秀威資訊科技, 2012.09
　　面； 公分. -- (語言文學類 ; PG0806)
　BOD版
　ISBN 978-986-221-986-7(平裝)

874.57　　　　　　　　　　　　　　　　　101015289

讀 者 回 函 卡

感謝您購買本書,為提升服務品質,請填妥以下資料,將讀者回函卡直接寄回或傳真本公司,收到您的寶貴意見後,我們會收藏記錄及檢討,謝謝!

如您需要了解本公司最新出版書目、購書優惠或企劃活動,歡迎您上網查詢或下載相關資料:http:// www.showwe.com.tw

您購買的書名:_____

出生日期:_____年_____月_____日

學歷:□高中 (含) 以下　　□大專　　□研究所 (含) 以上

職業:□製造業　□金融業　□資訊業　□軍警　□傳播業　□自由業
　　　□服務業　□公務員　□教職　　□學生　□家管　　□其它____

購書地點:□網路書店　□實體書店　□書展　□郵購　□贈閱　□其他

您從何得知本書的消息?

　□網路書店　□實體書店　□網路搜尋　□電子報　□書訊　□雜誌
　□傳播媒體　□親友推薦　□網站推薦　□部落格　□其他_____

您對本書的評價:(請填代號　1.非常滿意　2.滿意　3.尚可　4.再改進)

　封面設計____　版面編排____　內容____　文/譯筆____　價格____

讀完書後您覺得:

　□很有收穫　□有收穫　□收穫不多　□沒收穫

對我們的建議:_____

_____

_____

_____

11466
台北市內湖區瑞光路 76 巷 65 號 1 樓

秀威資訊科技股份有限公司 收

BOD 數位出版事業部

....

（請沿線對折寄回，謝謝！）

姓　　名：_____　年齡：_____　性別：□女　□男

郵遞區號：□□□□□

地　　址：_____

聯絡電話：(日) _____ (夜) _____

E-mail：_____